America's Mind

America's Mind

✫ ✫ ✫

Tim Avants

iUniverse, Inc.
New York   Bloomington

America's Mind

iUniverse books may be ordered through booksellers or by contacting:

iUniverse
1663 Liberty Drive
Bloomington, IN 47403
www.iuniverse.com
1-800-Authors (1-800-288-4677)

Because of the dynamic nature of the Internet, any Web addresses or
links contained in this book may have changed since publication and
may no longer be valid. The views expressed in this work are solely those
of the author and do not necessarily reflect the views of the publisher, and
the publisher hereby disclaims any responsibility for them.

ISBN: 978-1-4401-5732-5 (sc)
ISBN: 978-1-4401-5733-2 (ebk)

Printed in the United States of America

iUniverse rev. date: 07/01/2009

Chapter 1
Destined

There's something about a man that doesn't know who he is. Seems like when tragedy hits, he rewrites his thinking. He's a weak man, with no direction and no purpose. He's always changing. He's the kind of man that runs about looking for answers ...following this one or that one ...just whoever promises the best deal.

On the other hand, there's the type of man that knows exactly who he is and exactly what he was made for. This is the one who made America.

Ten years ago....

"You can do it! This is where champions are made! All the rest of 'em are at home right now. They THINK they did their work for the day. A REAL champion is working while the others are at home on the couch. He's doing windsprints while they're eating friggin' potato chips."

Dad was holding the bodybag, with his arms wrapped thru the handles on each side. Every time Bryce would hit it, sweat would fly onto his dad. The two were inseparable. This was the making of a champion…a Dallas Golden Gloves champion.

"Step into it ," he yelled. Spit shot from dad's mouth. Bryce bent deep to the left, and came from the hips, crushing two left hooks, 'doubling up' they called it.

" Now when you come up this next time, jab, jab, left, double up, weave right, then overhand right."

Brycie did it, then ended with a flurry of four punches.

He was ready.

Today….

Ssssssssssssssssseeeooow, ping! A bullet soared just to the left and hit the wall behind him. Two AL Qaeda were positioned across the street. Brycie and his two buddies had chased the two for ten blocks after they tried to kidnap a local woman.

�֎   ✖   ✖

"Brycie, he's just behind that jeep at 9 o'clock." Teddy waved to the left and let go a burst. It was returned by numerous bursts and then a rain of over 100 bullets, showering the whole area. Brycie and the other two hunkered down. Then silence. 1..2..3..the time was ticking. Nothing..nothing..nothing.

An eerie quiet...

The air cut ....ssshhhheeeooowww.. BBB uu UUUUFFF!! Teddy was shattered by a mortar...only pieces. He was gone. Another two or four by best he could tell had come in from the right.

✳   ✳   ✳

Only two of 'em left.

"Robie!!...." Brycie yelled.

"Yeah"...He was to the right and behind Bryce. ..between Bryce and the others with the mortar.

Another 5 or 6 bursts of machine gun fire hailed. Then thunderous hits all around Robie....Robie was stuck in between a mound of dirt and a wall. A perfectly accurate mortar round could relegate him to Teddy's fate.

"Im gonna move to my left. Cover me. "

The year before Golden Gloves....

Ding! ...end of round one...the first fight in an excellent boxing career...

Brycie made his way back to the corner and sat down. A strong young man of 16 years. His daddy had been a boxer, and his daddy, and his brother was too...a family who knew the truth.

"Ok, son, you're doing good. You got some blood and judges don't like to see that." Dad wiped the blood from his nose gave him water. Bryce was panting. The round was even. Maybe Bryce had edged him a bit. But this was a hometown boy in front of hometown judges in Troup, Texas...a small town of only five thousand at most.

"Listen to me..you gotta press him. Don't let him

friggin' breathe !! Up and down ! Up and down !! Come out smoking."

Round two. They stood toe to toe. They forgot the boxing because it was a slugfest, they both knew one with the most heart would walk away with the trophy today. They kept pounding back and forth, both bleeding, and the crowd was on its feet. Each and every person had a favorite. The townies loved the other boy and they were screaming his name.

The referee was a local, too.

Ding. Round two was over.

"Ok bubba, you're doing excellent. You hafta move your head though." Bryce nodded. " Now he's getting tired. Press him. Run thru him like a mack truck! You gotta win this round."

Round three. They walked out and touched gloves. The boy was panting, mouth open, hands down. For every one the boy threw, Bryce came with two or three. The boy was hurt and running outta gas.

"Sprint it out!" Dad yelled.

Bryce opened up and started hitting him with some powerful shots. ...just like sprints-as hard as he could as fast as he could.

The opponent started simply defending and going thru the motions. He'd paw out a jab and then move backward or to the side. He was trying to strategize and box. The boy didn't understand one thing: Sometimes you simply have to fight.

✳   ✳   ✳

Bryce began to overwhelm him and with every flurry, the boy would turn to the side. Even the referee, who was also a local, started to jump in and stop the pummeling. Then he would allow the fight to continue rather than stop the bout.

End of round three. Split decision. The other boy wins the bout.

Bryce, his dad, and older brother made their way out of the ring. A white boy cut thru the crowd, ignored the father, and reached out and grabbed Bryce by the hand.

"Hey man, you won that fight. I don't know what's wrong with those idiot judges. Then again, I think he's from here."

"Yo, thanks, man."

He held the disappointment in and wiped the sweat from his face. He had blood trickling from his nose again and he wiped it with his shirt. A couple of girls were looking at him with silly inexperienced eyes, noting the bad decision but more impressed with the muscular ridges in his stomach.

Three more fighters claimed he was robbed of the decision in the next few minutes, congratulating him on such a good fight.

✳   ✳   ✳

kekekekeke

The machine guns rattled away, tearing apart everything around Bryce. He put his head down. Concrete fell around him, big chunks blasted from the nearest wall.

It was almost continuous. He could hear his dad's voice. "You were made for this, son. From the beginning of time, this was destined to happen."

Another succession of shots thundered.

"Brycie !!!"

Robie was hit.

"Brycie !!...I'm hit!"

Again, the bullets ripped everything around Robie.

On the other side, the Iraqis were laughing. Bryce could hear their Arabic.

"Kalb! (Dog) Damn weak Americans. They come here to get us and we fuck them. Ha Ha! We fuck your women and children too!"

They laughed again.

He heard his dad again: "Don't let him breathe."

Brycie jumped up and let off a volley that took out the mortar. ..spraying the whole area. Two fell out and into the street. The mortar rolled into the street between them.

He hunkered down again.

Now he could hear yelling from the Arabs. They were pissed.

"Brycie !! Brycie !!!"

"Yo, man , just wait. I'll be there. "

He jumped up and caught a glance of the area. He didn't see anyone but figured they were playing possum. No sounds. He didn't hesitate but scrambled from his position and sprinted toward Robie. That was a 30 yard run. 15 yards into it, he became an open target. Three Iraqis stood up and opened fire. They sprayed continuously. His old days of wind sprints and gutting it out paid off. He jutted to the left and the men yelled as they fired fill throttle. A bullet nicked his heel but he kept running. Robie peeped up and squeezed his trigger. One Al Qaeda fell. Bryce threw a grenade and the explosion ripped thru their position, killing everyone.

It was still early in the day.

Chapter 2
The Influx

I enlisted at a young age to get a good future. Papa was a working man. He worked down at the Tyson plant most of his life. Hell, everybody I know worked there at one time or 'nother. It's kindly like a rite of passage round those parts. Papa done his time in the army and that helped him buy a home. I did my stint in Korea just like Papa. It beats sitting on a line all day ever day. When I was a lil kid, mama'd say stuff like I was gonna grow up and be somebody important. Ah, I guess...if this military life is what you call important.

I knew that I'd never do too much. I'm just a working man. I learnt my trade..mechanics.. in the army. And here I am now. It was free. Got me a 2 year old and a four year old. I do know one thing for sure--I'd rather be home.

But that don't matter none. What I want don't matter to nothing. When I was a boy, papa'd take us snake hunting. We had a farm up there kinda in the mountains of Arkansas...not too far from town but it was nice and off by itself though. Papa used to say that we had to kill any snakes that we saw within 100 feet from the house or else they'd be at our backdoor 'fore too long. I guess he was right cuz one summer he busted his leg and couldn't go out. I swear there at least 20 of 'em on the porch that summer, maybe more.

That's kindly the way we look at coming over here. They already done been to the US blowing up crap. And we just followed 'em back over to their nest. One year, papa took us up on the hill next to the house. He carried a can of kerosene, a shotgun, and me and my little brother. Halfway up 'er he said he found a nest of moccasins. Those damn water moccasins 'll flat out be aggressive. You aint gotta get in their territory. You let 'em go long enough and they'll take over a whole area. And they will kill you. It don't take nothin but a wrong step. In fact, granpa told me he knew a guy that stepped on a dead one and got killed.

I guess they can be poisonous even when theyre dead. There's too much poisonous crap in America these days. Too many friggin wetbacks comin over here takin our jobs.

In the past five or ten years, seems like the whole town's been taken over by spics. They're like cockroaches runnin' round everywhere and breedin'. My cousin lives up in

Rogers-just outside of town bout 15 miles or so and works at a Tyson plant. Small community. Maybe 15,000 people. Tyson hired all these Mexicans to come in and work. Man, now they got a new house with a big $20,000 car and they are everwhere. I got a friend whose boy went up there for work and they told him there full up. That dont make no sense cuz they was hiring on the radio. In fact, another friend of mine works for a siding company and the owner fired almost ever single American on the job and replaced 'em with wetbacks. They aint got no fuckin papers neither. That means instead of payin' him like $12 per hour, the owner's payin' 'em like $8 or $10 and then they'e here gettin free crap for immigrants. With these new laws that the hospitals caint turn nobody away, they're goin' broke. Two of 'em recently went bankrupt down near Laredo--on the American side.

And how in the hell can they come here on a work visa or even illegal for that matter and drop a kid and stay!! I been around the world workin and this is the only country in the world that does that--lets 'em drop a baby and stay here free. Then they's equal to you and me...and they aint done shit to get what they got. They piggybacked on my daddy's coattails-and mine too. Its a sight..just plain pitiful.

My son had a fight at school with one of 'em. They was all talkin' and someone said,' "We needta let 'em in cuz they do the jobs that Americans don't want to do." Who said? **Who said Americans don't wanna do them** *jobs?* Damn. My daddy worked at Tyson. I worked at Tyson. Now my son caint work there cuz they was full up. That's shit.

Up 'er in Danville, there 'r a million friggin' illegals. I saw a thing on TV and this guy went to the local hangout where they was all waiting for work. It was labor on a construction site. He couldn't get not one mexican to work for $12 per hour. Hell I got a brother that does home improvement for $12 an hour-and he's been on the job for at least ten years. Lot of 'em women 'll fuck an American and get his cash and then try to get married. Or they'll just drop a kid like I say. These women are beautiful and that's their way into the US. Then they get a divorce.

✳   ✳   ✳

Somebody needs to change the law about free citizenship. But a working man like me aint got no way to do that. Gots to be done at the polls. These friggin liberal faggots are given away the farm and a working man like me's gotta pay for it. I'm payin' for the health care and the taxes that they don't pay and the baby that's born here free and the welfare they get afterward.

People 'll say "but them mexicans will work." They say, man, "they's some hard workers." Bull shit. Mexico even totally and completely shuts down in the middle of the day for a "siesta." That means sleep! They close business to go home and go to sleep! People talk about "let foreigners keep their customs!" If we do, they'll be knockin" off of work to go home and go to sleep! They dont work no harder than anyone else. And besides, what an insult on all Americans every friggin where! Who in the hell-fire made America what it is today? Why in hell we all of a sudden need a bunch of friggin foreigners livin next door to us doin our jobs? Americans work !! Since when do we need a bunch of strangers comin in here and doin our work for us !! That's complete and total crap. I mean damn!! Hillary Clinton's talking bout how poor Americans are and can't afford health care!! Why in the hell are we inviting another country's poor people to come in here and work!! They makes no sense at all!!

And yeah they'll work for a lil while. Figure it like this. If the average middle class income for an educated man with a degree in Mexico is $600 per month, and it is, and they come over here and make $1200 per month doin pure labor, and that's for the uneducated farmers who were pickin crap for a livin' before they came here, then that's the same as you or me makin' $45 on the line at the chicken factory or diggin a ditch somewhere or at WalMart...But that second generation is who doesn't work. The girls get pregnant at 16, maybe 1 outta 5. The boys join gangs...etc. And I gotta pay for it. Congress wants to cut corners, but they needta cut the immigrant visas.

Now we let em all i8n n the economy went bad-not cuzza Bush but cuzza outsourcin' and givin the farm away. As a result, we gotta millions of immigrants in here and our own brothers and sisters cant find work. Then we got the pull on hospitalizing them and takin care of them. It's a vacuum.

Hell, I'd look busy all the day long-shoot-KEEP busy for that kinda money diggin a ditch. That means they make a week's salary from mexico in a day or two. A paralyzed man at the waist will get out and work labor for that kinda money. So toutin' the glory of the mexicans who come over here and eat our food, take our jobs, and fuck our teenage daughters is not a smart thing to do cuz there ain't no truth in it-they do just that-take the jobs and fuck our teenage daughters and then create friggin' ghettos and low riders and the second generation sells drugs.

Most of 'em 'll work the first generation. They got to or else not eat. but its all under the table mostly anyway. Maybe one 'll get sponsored and then there'll be 10 or 15 livin' in one apartment. They sneak em over here and then give em a place to stay. And then most of em don't try to fit in.

Papa always told me, "Son, git in where you fit in."

In the city...

The music pounded so loud that you could feel it in your stomach. "...low rider...don't use no gas now...." It was the Hispanic anthem in the US. The great American Midwest. Denver, Colorado. Just west of Colfax Avenue. Todd and his wife had just returned home from the market.

✳   ✳   ✳

"Todd, you know I cant cook spicy stuff."

"Look woman," he teased, "you'll cook spicy and that's that."

He chuckled a bit and reached over and tickled her in the ribs. She laughed and rearranged her grip on the bag. He loved it when she was vulnerable.

They could hear the music making its way up the street.

"Low rider, don't drive too fast now...da da da da du, da da da du, da...du..duuu..."

They were riding four deep.

That morning...

Mama was angry again.

"Mijo! I told you! You gotta help me around the house. Whatju doin' all day?...every day? Mi Dios! Todos los dias, no trabajo, cervesa, and I theenkju smokeeeng somtheeng too !! Why joor eyes alway red??!!"

Her tone was whiney but sharp and drawn out simultaneously. 11am on a Wednesday. Carlos rolled over and kicked a leg outta the bed. He stank like weed and liquor.

"Mama, stop ragging on meee. I'm not workeeeng

some stupeed job for minimum wage. I goin to make some reeal money."

She was in the kitchen on her way out.

"Ju know, Mijo, I very shame for you. You donn do notheeng. You eat and sleep and never come home. Ju twenny year old now. Do sometheeng with joor life. Es a geef from our God. I so lucky to have clean houses for money. I dont get notheeng else but the food stamp. ...and thank Dios beeecause I no taxes from my paid."

He stammered a bit and then bit his tongue. His head hurt and he needed a joint to take off the throb.

She continued, "But ju, ju a ceetizen here. You can go into thee military and help thees contree."

He lost it.

"To hell with this country. I am not a American ! I am Mexican."

"Ju are Mijo. You were naturalize."

"Fuck that! Fuck these people! Fuck this country! I don't give a damn about notheeng here ! ...and I aint working no frigging fast food restaurant. I aint gonna die for some frigging white conos! What they ever do for me!?!"

He could have stabbed her with a knife and it wouldn't've hurt any more than that.

"Aaaah..." Shame and dishonor and hurt and disappointment and sadness rent her heart.

"....mijo, mijo..oh, mi Jesus Cristo..toma su corazon... Jesus ..Jesus..."

✻　　✻　　✻

That aterrnoon...

At the east end of downtown, in the late afternoon, while 78% of Americans age 18-25 in the greater Denver area were either at work or in class, Carlos sat around in an abandoned garage apartment with three of his buddies. They were completely high. They had two blunts under their belt and now a duster.

Tiny was the smallest but had the biggest mouth. They said he had heart because he would fight anyone anywhere...they failed to think that was only when his buddies were there. And the other one was always outnumbered.

He tore into his sandwich like a rabid dog tearing at some meat...but he stopped long enough to take a drag and pass it on.

"Yo, Carlos, maaan, we gonna go do some work in a meeenit if you down weeth it."

He looked Carlos up and down and then cocked his head back and scrutinized his demeanor. Carlos knew 'work' meant he'd have another stripe by the end of the day. ..if he played it right. Carlos looked at him and inhaled as deep as he could, holding, holding, holding til he felt a rush, and then he exhaled. Carlos nodded and Tiny smiled and leaned back.

"See, Carlos," Tiny continued, "me and Tonio and Berto theenk you got what it takes to make some money."

✻　　　✻　　　✻

Carlos looked him in the eye and nodded again. Silence meant tough-here at least. A big mouth meant tough-out there at least.

"But we dooon know if you got the cajones to stand up like a soldier. You got to prove yourself. I know you wanna peeck one o these ladies here too!"

He pointed with his head to a sofa full of females. All of them were underage. Everyone in the room had already had sex with everyone else in the room-male-female that is. So that wasn't in and of itself a big attractive feature. He just wanted another stripe-the rest of the stuff came with the stripe.

"Get straight, ese, cuz we gonna do that theeng in a lil bit."

Tonio got up and grabbed one of the girls by the hand and went into an old nasty, smelly bathroom. Berto went and sat between the other two girls.

Tiny continued, "See, ese, we gonna hit this liquor store tonight. This fuckin' gook in theeere got a lotta Benjamins. I seen it. I dunno but maybe a thousan or somtheeng."

Carlos nodded again and leaned in a bit.

"Let's do it, ese, "Carlos said. "I hate fuckeeng gooks anyway. They some dirty mutherfuckers."

6:04 pm

Todd's wife turned out of curiosity and watched them coming up the street. ... 22 mph...slowly..steadily...the bass reverberated ..boom..boom..the rims glistened in the early evening sunlight. The sky was clear and Todd's wife was still flirting. As the car passed parallel, all four stared hard at Todd and his wife. The car slowed down to about 15... crawling along. Berto was driving with Tiny on shotgun. Carlos was in the rear driver's side, facing the side of Todd and his wife, and Tonio was on rear right side.

Todd was a man, a real man, and he looked back, not invitingly, but defensively. It was his property. He was there before the neighborhood went down and would be there after the riff raff had moved out.

"Hey, yo," Tiny said, "he think he a tough son a beetch. Stop! "Stop the fuckeeng car !"

Berto hit the brake and came to a dead stop.

"Back up, mother fucker!"

He eased back slowly, maybe 15 yards til the car was once again parallel to Todd and his wife.

Carlos felt it take him over. He had seen it before and now it was his turn. He could earn two stripes in one day. Carlos leaned out the window.

"Hey mother...fucker..whatju lookeeng at !!"

Todd pushed his wife away and she made her way into the house and peeked out the window.

"Mind your business!" Todd yelled back fully composed.

"Smoke that motherfucker."

"Yeah, man," Tonio started laughing, "He dissing you, man. Don't let that white ass mother fucker disrespect you, maaaan."

He drew out the 'man' for emphasis.

Carlos reached into his coat and pulled out a pistol.

Todd reached behind his waist and pulled out a pistol.

The two drew exactly the same time. Todd leveled and fired two times, striking the same area twice within an inch of each other. Tonio was taken by surprise because he had expected Todd to back down.

Tiny had his gun out and was trying to reach around Berto who was also stunned into inertia. Todd saw Tiny and ran up to within five feet of the vehicle. By that time, Tiny was pointing directly at Todd. Todd squeezed off two more rounds that struck Tiny in the chest and the throat. He slumped over, and the car sped away.

Todd got the license plate.

Thank God for his concealed weapon permit.

The law was successful.

Chapter 3
The Covering

The three had been inseparable for about a year or so. Most of the friendship was based in a so-called outreach ministry. This in and of itself was a good idea and helped a lot of people. With Rose, it started with rides to church because she didn't drive and she was a faithful one every chance she got. She had made up her mind to raise her boys in the fear and admonition of the Lord Jesus Christ. The relationship quickly diminished into a mentorship between Stacy and Rose. Stacy was poised to teach everything she knew about the evil of the male of the species and the 'equality' of the women.

Rose was a new Christian, recently baptized and had given herself to the Lord, full of questions and the joy of the Lord. She was a gullible girl, though not a girl, a woman of 26 years old. She had two small sons, Bryce and Duran. Bryce would later become a war hero. Both were excellent children. She was a brown woman, as she called herself, though society called her 'black.' The only distinction in her mind was that of color, and rightfully so. The correct term, the politically correct term, one that flutters about like a leaf in Autumn, was African-American.

Rose was not, however, as she was so quick to point, neither African, nor black, so that left her with the self-description of brown and American. Never one to give in to the semantics of terms, she would surprise all that knew her by giving in to the seduction of enfranchisement. This in turn was a nice name to disguise disruption, interference, and emasculation in the home. Not that all disruption is not warranted, but the break of sin and the grasp thereof is always warranted. One could only wonder at what cost it is.

Abigail was an excellent woman. She came from a good white, middle-class family. Her father worked at a business and her mother was a stay-at-home mom. She went to public school in the small town of Edmond, Oklahoma but now lived in Oklahoma City. She had raised three children and sent them off to school. Now at 46, her life had a vacant spot, both in time and in self-fulfillment. She was active in the church. She knew right from wrong, and shied away from any appearance of evil. Attractive as she was, men seemed to avoid making advances to her simply because they could sense the goodness in her. She was a righteous woman. This was not a righteousness of works but one of faith. She had accepted Jesus as her Lord and Savior at the tender age of 16. She was never touched inappropriately but gave herself to her covering on her wedding night. Like any other marriage, they had had their problems, as the old phrase goes, but through her dedication and sacrifice, they had been successful in the marriage and in the raising of their children. All that knew her called her blessed.

Michael (pronounced Mi-kae-ul) was a seemingly good woman, too. Her middle name Stacy was the one she was called by yet she still carried the spirit of Saul in her, one that raises itself through self-proclamation and feeds on the power of political correctness. However, she was always at church-twice on Sunday, and Wednesday nights, as well. She had opened a business at an older age. Now, at 47, she felt complete. She had a good husband. He was good to her, and she loved him. She had had a troubled marriage before -to a drinker. He had hit her, to what extent no one is really sure. But she had divorced and remarried seven years earlier. Inside, she retained the bitterness, stuck away like a trophy to be revealed only to a limited few and only to legitimize certain behavior and ideas that might otherwise appear unseemly. Nevertheless, she did some good for some people some of the time. In short, her presence in the second pew on the left side of the sanctuary every time there was church was enough to convince the world that she was a good Christian with a good heart. Her righteousness was one of self and one of works.

As service in the ministry would have it, many occasions were had to fellowship one with another. Every opportunity that presented itself, Rose seized upon to do what she could in the service of the church. And either Stacy or Abigail would provide the ride for Rose. But with Rose's new found friends and her realization that she was indeed 'equal,' she also learned that there were many local government agencies that could help her in her effort to emancipate herself from her husband, get financial assistance, and become free. This freedom, she was so convinced, was one of inner spirit, that because she was in the United States of America, and because she was a child of God, she need not submit to the edicts of a man who didn't faithfully attend service, as well. This of course was the result of many asides...

Wednesday night, 6:45 pm, en route to Liberty church in Edmond, Oklahoma...

"i just don't really know how to handle it. He comes home at night and the very first thing he does it pop open a beer. Then he lies down on the couch and drinks about ten right up until he falls asleep right there."

Stacy looked at her sideways and bent her mouth in condemnation.

"Honeychild, you do not have to put up with that. A man should be at church with you. He needs to be leading those kids and doing whatever …

..ANYTHING except sitting around drinking all night."

Rose sat for a minute and then continued. She relished the attention. Actually, the attention was the only thing that ever made her feel important.

"...and I think he cheats on me."

This was the open door for Stacy. ...super Stacy to the rescue.

'aaaah, no he doesn't !! How do you know that? That's the one thing in the Bible that you never ever have to accept. That is the one grounds for divorce-other than being abandoned."

Rose sat back for a minute and soaked up the rattling invective against ungodly husbands...listening to the recollections of a woman done wrong, saturated with bitterness and self adulation, purportedly found at the cross and the cleansing of the blood. But in reality, though Stacy believed, she was driven by hate, a child who had never recovered from rejection, bound and determined to right the wrongs in every other marriage she could get her hands on...or in. As the months went by, Stacy and Rose formed a special bond. Their friendship turned into teacher and student. Rose would soak up the bittersweet advice from Stacy and the embellished stories from Rose turned into a magnet for pity. On this Rose thrived. On that she built her plan for escape. On the other things that went with it she made alliances in the church.

The lukewarm believer without had become the target from those within.

After church one night, the ladies fellowship group had a potluck. This was the norm once or twice per month. All those who wanted gathered to eat for a small fee designated for a special fund such as the church teen camp or homeless missions.

Rose was at the table and a young black man made his way from across the room. He had some information about her marriage and she made an easy mark so he gathered. This was the black snake looking for something to devour. His was a 'Christian rap.'

"Hello, sister."

She stood back for a minute and automatically set up a barrier.

"Hello. Good service tonight. You usually don't come on Sunday nights," Rose said.

"Yeah, well, I have to work."

He was clean and dressed like a man on a mission...a little too clean for a Sunday night. He reached over and helped her pour some punch and then handed her the glass. She knew what he wanted, why he came up to her, and what he was. But she let her guard down for just a minute. They talked for a minute or two and he was in. She felt pretty. He felt victorious-almost.

"...Where's your husband?"

"He never comes. He's at home drinking right now. I'm sure of it."

"Don't you have kids? ...a couple of boys, I think." He memorized details like that.

She was flattered. "I do. How did you know that?"

"Sister, I can't help but notice...things like that." The 'sister' was a double edged sword-black and Christian. She wanted to be black at that minute.

As time passed, their friendship grew. Funny thing, a crack in the door can make the pressure blow the door completely off its hinges. It led to sin.

She rarely fought fair anymore.

"Well all you do is sit around and drink !!"

"All I want is for the house to be clean. That's it! You're at home all friggin' day with nothing to do...and you can't even clean the damn bathroom?!"

✳   ✳   ✳

"I am not your maid! I am your wife...I shouldn't have to be running behind you cleaning up and picking up your smelly beer cans !"

It erupted further back and forth and she spit in his face and then lit into him like a man, swinging wildly. They went to the floor, while she was scratching and biting like a cat with distemper. He managed to pin her hands. She stopped, and spit in his face again from the bottom position. He let her up.

✳   ✳   ✳

The next day when he got home, she was gone. He was the worst man in Edmond, according to Liberty church, and she was the battered wife.

✳   ✳   ✳

A man and a woman should never separate, some believe. It opens the door for others...and it did. He met a girl during the separation. Actually, she had just disappeared on him one day with no word, taken the kids and that was that. He was left alone. Eventually there was reconciliation though. They moved in together once again and started over.

✳   ✳   ✳

She never admitted anything. He went against his old motto, "Never admit nothin'." Over time his heart changed. And as he spent more and more time with the Lord, he completely changed. He was no longer the man she married. At that point in his life, wife gone, children gone, he cried out, "God change my heart!"

✳   ✳   ✳

This man who had proclaimed for years and years that he would never, ever change had indeed changed. Not that he had been a particularly bad man before. He was honest. He tried to do the right thing. But in her exuberance when she became saved, she began to condemn and condescend to him. Her disposition was wielded like a weapon. She begged him, "Please, please repent before you die and go to hell! You're no kind of example for these boys. We are ashamed of you. "

This was not so bad but the accompanying judgments that he was not worthy of her and he was a terrible father pushed him, so to speak, to a point of vulnerability. With her gone, and with another younger, prettier model making advances to him, he gave in. There is a point where a man, any person for that matter, won't tolerate judgment and condescension. People cannot clean themselves from iniquity, so where is the boasting? He knew the truth already and he believed. Yet a little beer here and a sideways glance there seemed to fuel the fires of condemnation that constantly spewed from the tongue of his wife. She had become a Pharisee, and it wasn't pretty. Neither was she. And feminist Stacy along with another ex-battered (we are led to believe) woman named Lilian provided monetary support and bad counsel every step of the way. The sting of feminism had made its way into the church body and it was like an infection.

So life together again plowed through the drudgery of every day. He admitted his indiscretion with the high yellow 19 year old and was supposedly forgiven. Time went by. Ten years. Fifteen years. She even said, "I forgive you."

✳   ✳   ✳

He couldn't believe the graciousness of his wronged wife. Actually he fell in love with her all over again because of her forgiveness. But forgiveness is not a thing that can be given and then taken back. People say that a word can never be taken back once it's spoken, then how much more true with two these words that break the bonds of hatred. But the good times were few after that. The nasty, filthy comments were made and her heart turned into stone.

Then, a living bitterness took root. One that had life and substance and form and even character. It was not like hurt that many females carry on their chest as a badge of courage but one that was tucked away inside, growing a little every day, sometimes escaping through the mouth amidst white spittle to the left corner, taking the outline of words that were so undeniably nonsensical that anyone near would realize this bitterness was affecting her mental health. In short, her malice drove her crazy. Yet he endured. He took it. He had two young boys, born of a white father and a black mother-a "caucasoid" and a "negroid", as he jokingly referred to himself and his wife. For all of them, race had never been an issue…at least until the church women got involved. Things never changed with the boys. But to the rest of the world, he was the bad white man who abused the poor little black girl…and so it seemed.

A little leavening leavens the whole lot.

So it was, for years and years. He endured for the boys as she had in the past-for the children. He never cheated again. But a foolish woman will pluck down her house by her own hand. And she did. He stayed and used it as an opportunity to teach his boys. Above all, he wanted to be a good example to them. He knew that ,given the climate of marriage in the world at the time that, they might go through the very same thing. And they saw. And they learned. He taught them how to be real men. God first. Then family. Then country. He had given himself for his wife. He endured for their sake, so they might have a daddy. He taught them all he knew. And they carry it with them today.

God changed his heart. He submitted to the tugging of the Holy Spirit. He knew that he would never justify himself. That had already been done for him on the cross. She hated the world. Eventually he met someone new...a pharmacist, 13 years younger...an Asian woman. He remarried a younger, prettier, smarter woman who bore him a child. His new wife got the bed and the bread.

Rose's color faded, the sparkle in her eye was gone, and she became a wilted thing-all out of malice. She got a job as a waitress and moved to the Hispanic ghetto near her old house.

Chapter 4
The Contrast

7:53 P.M.
Overland Park, Kansas

"Well," he spouted to his lover as he pranced by and flopped himself on the couch, "they never found any weapons, and they need to just get outta there right now."

He rearranged his legs so his bis belly wouldn't interfere with his breathing.

"Anyway," he continued, "what the fuck do I care if they kill each other? Those sand niggers are all alike anyway..." he inflected his voice in his feminine distinctiveness. "...hell, honey, they've been killing each other for a thousand years."

His thin little lover named Stanley walked in front of him and sat beside him.

"I know," said the lover, "but we need to help those people. It IS our duty. Besides, they are all part of the same group that came right over here and blew up 3500 people."

It was unusual for the thin one to go against Charles. Charles had a temper, and he didn't mind displaying it. After all, he had little or no self control. His appetites led the way to his destruction.

Charles stared at him.

"Honey, we can't stop one single thing over there. They were killing each other before America even existed. And they'll be killing each other after we're gone."

The thin one felt a bit of boldness for a change. He had done research. He had kept up for 30 years.

"Actually", he hesitantly continued...waiting for an outburst..."

Iran had funded the Hezbollah to go into Lebanon during their civil war in the 1970s. This was after the Islamic revolution in 1976. That's the same time the Ayatollah took the American hostages. Shortly thereafter, the barracks were bombed in Beirut and over 2oo American marines were killed..."

Silence form Charles. He was listening although he pretended to be engrossed in the TV.

"Iran also is partly funding the insurgence in Iraq. It isn't only the Iraqi fundamentalists that we are fighting there now. They have created a political party in Lebanon and actually hold key posts in the country.

It is the antagonizing party that conducts cross-border raids against Israel-the same exact party that bombed the Marines, the same exact party that our traitorous ex-president Jimmy Carter went and met with, the same exact party that Barack Obama said he'd meet with-a TERRORIST party. They should've taken Carter's damn passport. In fact, the Ayatollah Khomeini of Iran supported the taking of the hostages during Carter's presidency AND the bombing of the 200 marines in Beirut by Hezbollah, and then his ass went and met with Hezbollah. If that's not being a traitor, then I don't know what is. And now Barack Obama says he will meet with them too! Are you gonna meet with people who already killed your family?"

He paused and then continued.

"Plus, maybe they didn't find the actual weapons themselves there, but they did find weapons making materials, and like Chuck said, 'Saddam Hussein was a weapon of mass destruction.'"

Charles looked at him.

"Who in the hell is Chuck?"

"Chuck Norris, silly."

"Ahhh", Charles relaxed again. "Oh, that's all damn bullshit..."

"Look, Saddam Hussein told the world that he was gonna build weapons of mass destruction. He gassed his

own people and killed them-men, women, and children..
which, by the way, is the SAFEST part of Iraq right
this minute. He attacked Kuwait and carried off men,
women, and children who were never heard from again.
He had torture chambers where thousands were tortured
to death-shocking their balls and lighting them on fire.
He fired scud missiles at Israel without any provocation
whatsoever-they had absolutely nothing to do with the
Gulf War and he tried to kill them. Just a good thing
that those scuds had no power. Why would he want a
more powerful weapon anyway? ...to actually hit his
target ! We did the right thing for sure. Besides, Osama
bin Laden sent a man to meet Saddam Hussein at the
end of the First Gulf War. See, Osama bin Laden had
been funding the insurgents inside of Iraq. In order to
stop the backing, Saddam agreed to let Osama set up
training camps inside of Iraq. Now we're talking as early
as 1992. We also know there were a series of bombings
in different embassies around that time. Osama sent his
man Zawahiri to Baghdad to set it all up. We don't know
what exactly what happened after that-only that Osama
did continue later on to support Iraqi insurgents. Those
same exact dissidents were still in

Iraq when we took out Saddam Hussein. That's who
we're fighting right this minute. We ARE still fighting in
Iraq the same ones who worked with Osama bin Laden to
blow up 911. Abu Musab al-Zarqawi, the one that led al
Qaeda in Iraq for so long, may also have been supported

by bin Laden in setting up Kurdish terrorists. Of course, the Kurds live in northern Iraq. The Kurds are ok but not Ansar al-Islam, the terrorist group. There's a clear link in all of it, but most people are too unknowledgeable to know what's goin' on."

"I ought to beat your ass." Charles was a pervert. They both were. But the thin one was still right.

He continued, "After all, what is the difference between there and, say, Rwanda when all the genocide was going on in 1992?"

Silence.

"Nothing. No difference at all. Well, I take that back. There is one difference: The extremists have tried to take us out and were even successful in downtown NYC. But if the world will go into Rwanda to stop the genocide, Iraq citizens are no less important. We helped stop the killing in El Salvador and Nicaragua too-all to stop the killing by murderous regimes. Would you let a guy kill an old lady or a kid on the street right in front of you?"

"Fuck them," Charles blurted.

"Now I know you don't mean one word of any of that. I know you better than that."

"Ok. Ok. Honestly, I'd go get some help."

"That's it, Charles, we ARE the help."

Charles was a coward. He always had been. He always was and always would be. That was part of his thinking, as well. He never told anyone. But he always thought, that if he acted feminine, he wouldn't be challenged to duels like men were. As time passed, he became a bully to the other smaller ones who shared his lifestyle. He cared about little else but immediate gratification. He wanted what he wanted when he wanted it. But his life had taken form as a young boy.

His parents had had no skills and no assertiveness as REAL parents. They threw the responsibility of Charles' well-being on the school counselors and psychologists and psychotherapists involved in Charles' very unusual childhood. At a young age, perhaps six, Charles always felt compelled to dress like a girl. He would tell his mother (his father didn't want to hear it) that God had made a mistake...that he should have been a little girl... that he WANTED to be a little girl.

His mother and father were average people. They were heterosexual. They went to work every day. The mother was a nurse and the father worked with investments. But they had no inner strength. They couldn't say no-at least the mother couldn't. The father didn't say anything at all. The father's way of dealing with the issue was to change the subject. He was a pussy. They had two other children. Charles would not relent though. He had a love of the frilly women's clothing. He liked heels and loved the very smell of cosmetics. Night after night, he would speak into the ear of his mother.

"Mommy, why did God make me like this? Mommy,

I want to wear a dress. Mommy, I'm sure that God made a mistake."

And from her ignorance, she spoke not.

Will the thing formed say of Him who formed it, 'He has no understanding'? And the mother allowed the god of this world to have his way, not the God of all heaven and earth. She sat in the counsel of the ungodly.

And the father betrayed his position as leader of the family unit and thereby betrayed his own flesh. The mother sinned against her child and her family and God. She listened to the babblings of a whore, and they turned 'things upside down.'

They didn't understand one thing: Charles was not MADE like that. She didn't understand that grace was given to each person as a measure of Christ's gift so that we may no longer be children, tossed to and fro and carried about with every wind of doctrine. Neither did she know that she was not contending against flesh and blood but against principalities and spiritual hosts of wickedness in heavenly places. But she had already opened the door.

His mother became more and more distressed as time went by. She caught him in her wardrobe numerous times. And these were not simple, childish acts like most kids delve into before having any knowledge of the world, but they were sincere cravings that Charles harbored and even fed through television and magazines. His mother would secretly buy him magazines and rent DVDs such as Rochelle/Rochelle. It could have stopped with her but she was ignorant. Like an educated brute beast, she knew nothing of nothing, only facts that helped her achieve the title of "professional." But that means nothing at all in relation to real life. In short, her weakness and ultimately that of his father, as well, led to the horrible life that Charles was would endure. And it was called "self-actualization."

One street over...

7:54 P.M.

Teddy's wife leaned over her son, and cut his pizza for him. Amanda was her name.

"Ok, Davey," she said, "Lean over your plate when you eat it. Mommy doesn't want a mess, ok?"

"Ok, mommy."

He looked like his dad. Blond hair. Green eyes. He was a good boy. And she was a good mother and wife. A patient woman. She was a small-town girl from Hayes, Kansas. A pretty woman at age 25, a wife, a mother, a full-time mother and full-time student. She met Teddy when he was on his Advanced military training in Hayes. He used to go into where she was working part-time and eat. They struck up a friendship and fell in love. After a year or so, they got married. Then Joey was born. Then at the onset of the Iraq War, he was called to active duty. After he had done his initial hitch, he remained in the Guard. His unit was one of the first to go. That left her alone with Davey. But she had family nearby who helped out. Amanda's mother would watch Davey when she went to class.

✳   ✳   ✳

Her mother and father were good Methodists from the Midwest. She had an excellent upbringing-mostly because her parents refused to give in to whatever was popular at the minute. They were conservative and proud of it. They came from the Bible belt. And they wore the Bible's teachings like a belt. They girded the Word about themselves. It upheld them and saw them through crisis after crisis. Another one of their children had been killed in a car accident years eight years earlier. That was Amanda's little sister. She was killed by a drunk driver at the tender age of 16. Amanda was 17 at the time and it took her months and months to recover. It destroyed her senior year in high school.

Her mother would say, "Amanda, honey, God doesn't make mistakes. He is Almighty and all powerful."

Amanda had a hard time understanding why God would take her little sister. They had so many plans. Her sister Grace was planning to be a doctor and spent hours and hours in the books. On a Friday night when all the other kids were out somewhere, she would have her head in a book. She was the smart one of the family.

One night weeks after the accident, Amanda was in her room sobbing for hours and hours. Her mother came in and sat on the bed. Amanda lay with face down in the pillow to quiet her sobs.

Her mother gently put her hand on Amanda and massaged slowly.

"Sweetheart, I know this is hard for you. It is hard for all of us, but let me tell you something. Ok?"

Amanda kept her head down.

"The Bible says that God knew Grace's name from the beginning of time. When she was a little baby and she almost died, I told God that I would dedicate her to Him if I could just have her and if He would just let her stay with us. And then all of a sudden, she got well and then she was with us for 16 wonderful years...."

Amanda sat up and turned toward her mom.

"I don't want to hear that anymore! It's not fair!"

She hit her pillow.

A tear coursed its way down the cheek of her mom.

"Oh honey, don't you know that all of this is just a gift?"

Amanda sat up and hugged her mom and they cried together.

Another street over...

Father and son sat on the couch of their living room. The boy was a 19 year old straight out of his first year in college. He had dropped out of school to join up... despite the protests of his parents. But he was a man now and he could make his own decisions. His father knew this day would come because he knew his son had been created to serve others. Over the years, the son seemed to be blessed with the understanding of TO WHOM MUCH IS GIVEN, MUCH IS REQUIRED.

The father knew his son would take the reins, so to speak, and lead the charge to protect the country because he himself had taught that to his son. It's inevitable, a man lives up to his teaching. His dad was a school teacher and his mother worked at the public library. They both understood the meaning of service. Service doesn't mean serving the special interests of a few over the goodness of the whole. Equal rights never rewrites morality. The laws of man can never rewrite the laws of nature.

Bobby understood all of these things because his father was there. His father stood there as a man teaching a boy-who would later take over the same responsibility. They knew what the Bible said about things and they followed it-strictly. These were not new times to the James family because Mr. James had been in the Vietnam War. He had served and saw the same type of carnage. He was an educated man. He knew his place in the world. Because of this, and this mainly, he lived a peaceful life. He lay down at night in peace and all that he put his hand to prospered. He also saw first-hand the responsibility of the American people. TO WHOM MUCH IS GIVEN, MUCH IS REQUIRED.

At 20 years of age, he had been drafted into the army and spent time in the bush. A year. He saw guys blown apart. Lost two best friends in the war. Then he saw the weakness of a president turn tail because of millions of spineless, dope-smoking kids who demonstrated on campuses around the country. He saw these kids whom had never worked a day in their lives turn the course of history through their protestations...and eventually cause the deaths of millions of people in Laos, Cambodia, and Vietnam because the American government pulled out of Vietnam.

In his heart, he swore he would never let that happen again. Voting was the way to ensure it didn't.

He knew that there was a definite vein of events that led to the cowardly heart of those who cried out for "accept, accept" and "peace, peace."

During the 1960s, the sexual revolution turned the bodies of countless young people into satan's playground. They cast their teachings aside for the titillation of sin. It was as if anything went. These were the same ones crying out for peace. They wanted the freedom of the American dream but they didn't want to contribute anything. Now those same ones are retiring from the post office and have grandchildren serving to defend not only their country but also others who cannot defend themselves. This revolution gave way to a radical feminism. Feminism tore down the boundaries between decorum and same sex unions. Not that no good came from women's equal rights. Equal pay was a right that stemmed directly from feminist's campaigning. But the ever pressing quest for "rights" led to the further expansion of what the word "rights" actually entails. It redefined nature. The gay "rights" movement gained momentum from the feminist movement, and now it remains a constant battle on the American landscape.

Unfortunately, the world incorrectly perceives the whole gay thing as an American thing. That is definitely a fallacy. In fact, most Americans find it disgusting. At most, the majority of Americans would say that THAT population should not be discriminated against, but there should be no special dispensation to allow gay unions. The issue's popularity comes through the media and its never-ending coverage of the related developments. Because America is a democracy, there are legal avenues to get a case heard. Other vectors of publicity come from those locations where perverse behavior has been the norm for ages-Hollywood, for instance. "Accept-accept" is a buzz phrase that preys on people's weakness. If one does not accept moral corruption and put a stamp of approval on it, s/he is declared a discriminator, a hater, a nationalist, or whatever negative term that hits him in the stomach until he gives in for the sake of his own reputation. But only the weakest give in. Morality is not something that can be rewritten and nature can never be countermanded. And a "man" can never bear a child.

"Son, I am proud of you."

Bobby left for one last night out with his friends. Time would pass and the corps would turn him into a real man. He would get married while he was in the service. And they would have a child. He picked up where his father had left off.

Mr. James picked up his Bible and started reading Romans 1: 22:

"Claiming to be wise, they became fools, and exchanged the glory of the immortal God for images resembling mortal man.... Therefore God gave them up in the lusts of their own hearts to impurity, to the dishonoring of their bodies among themselves, because they exchanged the truth about God for a lie and worshiped and served the creature rather than the Creator."

An earlier time...

Charles fidgeted in his seat as his mother talked to the psychologist. The psychologist leaned back in her chair and crossed her legs. Charles' father found her to be a striking woman, very appealing, almost as if she masked something which simmered constantly. He could hear her lid boiling.

"You see, Mr. and Mrs. Taylor, Charles is dealing with transgender conflict." She waved her hands about for emphasis. "He actually feels as if he is a female trapped inside a male body. Studies legitimize this sort of thing."

Mrs. Taylor wringed her hands for a minute and then spoke.

"We just want Charles to be happy. Uh...er.." Gasp. "...what can we do?"

"Well, you need to encourage Charles to explore **HIS** feelings. What can it hurt? He needs to feel his value as a human. Who is it that can say his feelings are not legitimate? By passing any sort of judgment or limits on his desires at this age, we are in essence negating his very inner being...."

Mr. Taylor jumped in.

"You mean, that we should say OK?"

Mr. Taylor didn't like the idea but he was never really a man. He was male but he never knew the truth about anything at all. To him, 2+2 = 4 was the truth. And that was good enough for him. He paid the bills, had sex with his wife, and went to church on Sundays. That was it.

Mrs. Taylor cleaned the house, got the kids off to school, did the shopping, and had sex with her husband. That was it. She had a little more spark in her quest for understanding. So she was a reader...constantly searching for a truth. And she found tidbits here and there. This study and that study. But to her, determining the truth was hard because this or that study always seemed to contradict the one prior. This fat helped that condition but too much had an adverse effect. One scientist said 'don't touch this' and the other one said 'that one was best.'

She recalled her old days at college and her class on Modernism. Everyone always searched for the truth but always seemed to fall short, catching a glimpse but never coming to the full understanding. This was no modernist novel. But she definitely felt like a modernist character.

Mr. Taylor was distracted by the underside of the psychologist's thigh. Her demeanor was so hard to figure out. His focus was always so clouded by such things. The doctor looked down at them, peering over the the top of her wire-frame glasses. She felt sophisticated. And how fulfilling it was to be able to lead those ignorant people in the right direction. Life was good.

The doctor's mind flashed back to her college days and the free-spirited times she had there. Free love, endless pot and the ability to do anything she wanted. Her stream of encounters seemed just as real now...and they were, because she always had new ones. She was desirable. Her husband had no idea either. She felt Mr. Taylor's caressing of her inner female with his greedy eyes and it was good. She felt sexy. She felt smart. She was in control. And she specifically felt smart in the respect that her job was not to impose a goal as it were...no specific destination. She only wanted Charles and his family to come to their own goal. Basically, whatever they decided was Ok. Whatever CHARLES decided to do or be was the hidden treasure. That was the center of this universe. And she was the god.

Mr. and Mrs. Taylor listened intently for the next 30 minutes. They had fallen prey, yea had given themselves over to be prey, to human philosophy and deceit. Charles knew only one thing in his closed universe-for as long as he could remember-although he was never touched by an individual, Nightly, he felt a presence that entered his room. It was as if something mounted him and stirred a desire...demonic. He never told anyone.

And so these sessions continued day after day, month after month and year after year. Always discussing.

Always rationalizing. He was important now and nothing else mattered but his wants and 'needs.' Charles was important. He was the most important one in the family. He was special. No one came before Charles. As he grew, he got bigger and bigger -over 200 pounds. He had a natural power, although he was still fat and slobbish. He learned that he could dominate those who had the same affliction as he. He could in essence rule a small pond while sating himself in the process.

His father went to the priest and was ordered to light a candle and to pray to a dead human. It didn't help. There's something about a man who has no foundation. He goes where he is told and does what he is told...and at the end, he has no idea where he is or how he got there. Such was Mr. Taylor.

Mr. Taylor had never stood up before and neither did he have legs to stand now. His child was consigned to hell on earth as a result. Past that, his future was just as certain.

A man most often does what he is taught. It's given to him as a child, from day one, and then it is told to him over and over again. When he steps out of line, he needs to be corrected, subjugated, and brought right back into formation. This is his upbringing, his coming of age. But coming of age is a process, one that is experienced over and over again.

But where there is no truth, he is taught by what he sees or what he happens to hear or what he happens to simply stumble across along the way. If he sees his father led about by the woman of the house, he'll probably be led about the same way. With no guidance, the child throws the tantrum in the market and the whole line is disrupted. The tail begins to wag the dog and the parameters of decorum are redrawn. This same small one that at the time seems somewhat innocuous becomes the one who scoffs at the law and the jurisprudence of co-existence.

We create our own little monsters that eventually devour us by never standing up. Someone will stand up somewhere with something. And that person will eventually lead if the others waffle about because of social pressure or ignorance or even plain fear. The question is simple-who will stand up first?

The sexual revolution was like an adulteress who crept in and established herself as the lady of the house. That behavior had gone on since the beginning but a little justification affected the mind of the married woman. Dinners at home gave way to the working wife, TV dinners, and affairs on the job. That in turn spilled over into the covert gay lifestyle. Then they said they wanted the same type of equality. They claimed to be the same as women with inherent equality. It took an immoral president who practiced adultery in the oval office to bring "alternative lifestyles" to the table of discussion. He never changed his thinking.

From there, the way was clear for official unions of same sex. And the dog watched as the little tail wagged it to and fro--bashing it against the wall and bruising it before the world at large. And the battle rages on still-only because the few with the truth at breast refuse to sit down.

A man goes by what he is taught.

The distinction of right and wrong in the western world is usually misunderstood by those with little knowledge of democracy. Though one perceives the "Christian" nation as decadent, the truth is otherwise. The separation of church and state disallows religion to be imposed through the law. Therefore, when the eastern world sees same sex unions, adultery, prostitution, and violence in the street, most assume it is a product of Christianity.

In fact, this is all the product of sin-plain and simple. But the law doesn't judge one's behavior on the definition of sin. To the law, sin is irrelevant. Archaic laws such as sodomy and adultery have been either stricken from the books or are simply ignored. What one does in private is that: private. Nevertheless, because people have the right to TRY to get organized and accepted, they have sought recognition in the court to be "equal" and "legitimate." This attempt by no means suggests that the majority of Americans accept or indulge in the same behavior.

In fact, this same president Bill Clinton was brought up on charges in the Senate-not because of adultery in the white House but because he had lied about having sex. That was his crime. And he narrowly escaped being kicked out of office. Why? Because the same ones who won the vote to not kick his ass out were the Democrats. They don't vote for morality but for the sake of money. Their main constituency are poor people. Therefore, the poor people accept (usually) this deplorable and despicable behavior because a Democratic president gives away free abortions, free lunches, and free health care. Their morality is attached to money. They have sold their heritage for a bowl of porridge. But that is not the majority-though the numbers sway back and forth and it always depends on the economy. But regarding adultery and unnatural sexual behavior, most Americans don't want it anywhere around them. Only a small percentage engage in it-at least openly. They know that it is wrong and try to hide it.

The feeling of the populace is this: Leave them alone as long as they keep things legal.

Just because something is not illegal does not mean it is not immoral.

And they continue...unfettered-in every society under the sun. Yet here, in the land of milk and honey, it is perceived as the norm because we are the most powerful nation in all of history. The publicity comes from the small few that seek to publicly shame those who speak up for morality. The small percentage of those who openly support same sex marriage try to shame the ones who speak out against homosexuality and open immigration. The best way to shut someone up who has the right to speak is to shame him. But how can one be shamed and brought into dishonor for refusing to accept what is wrong?

To the foreigner, the whole American landscape appears like a big city-a metropolis that functions as one, coherently and cohesively, each part working together for the good of its people. Yet in actuality, the American landscape is made up of alliances that come together to gain their own agenda. They are like battling neighborhoods. Gay marriage advocates are usually allied with heterosexual abortionists who want "abortion on demand." Separately, they are very weak, but together they are a strong foe. Then, to accept one usually means to accept all. They in turn are in bed with proponents of open immigration. They would open the border if they could. In addition, this lot will not fight if attacked. They run from defending their own country. The same president who committed adultery in the white house in his office also vetoed a ban on partial-birth abortion. Nothing at all was required to perform partial-birth abortion except the permission of a doctor. no life-threatening illness or condition, no pending doom, no, nothing at all was required to perform this procedure. So Republican President George W. Bush immediately banned this legal murder when he took office.

This killing was banned by Congress but the President has the right to veto a ban. Bill Clinton's veto had done this: it allowed the mother to induce labor as late as 8 or 9 months. When the child came out of her body, one of two procedures would be performed to kill the child. The doctor would either insert a needle at the base of the baby's skull or put a pair of forceps over the skull and crush it. Clinton's voters also supported same sex marriage. To allow the one is to allow the sum.

Our city is unequally yoked. There is godly grief in only one neighborhood. Only one neighborhood had real teaching. And there is no room for heresy. Godly grief produces a repentance that leads to being saved and brings no regret, but worldy grief produces death.

Chapter 5
Small Town Boy

If with Christ you died to the elemental spirits of the universe, why do you live as if you still belonged to the world? Why do you submit to regulations, "Do not taste, Do not touch" (referring to things which all perish as they are used), according to human precepts and doctrines? These have indeed an appearance of wisdom in promoting rigor of devotion and self-abasement and severity to the body, but they are of no value in stopping the indulgence of the flesh.

My name is Donny Sims. I was born and raised in Akron, Colorado-a small town of 1800 people. My mother was a nurse at the local hospital and my father worked at and retired from the Highway Department. That was a real hard job given the hard winters that we have. My brother Danny worked at the local feed mill for 21 years. He's married and has three kids. I have a little boy, 6, and a little girl, 4. My favorite song is that John

Mellencamp one about the small town-I can't remember the name.

I was in the National Guard to get money for school and then we were mobilized. I did two years in Sterling at the community college and worked at the auto parts store. Sterling is really considered a medium size city to most of us. It has about 15,000 people. I'm glad that I can come over here and help these people because they are mostly just hard-working people like we are. I mean, they have a different religion and all but they get up and go to work like everyone else does. It's just that these nuts get into power and pillage the whole countryside. They have different customs, of course, but every place is different in how they carry out the same type of stuff.

I try to think if I were here and people came busting in on my family and took what they wanted and even took me or my father--forever. Lots of people just disappear. The thing is, it's the people in power who do it. So who can you go to for help if the police are the ones who come in and take away your father or brother? The women are pretty much guarded and kept under lock and key but it seems like most all else is fair game. I have personally seen the torture chambers. I know that Saddam's two sons used to just take a woman anytime they wanted. So that means this little virgin girl might be seen by one of them and he'd just send for her. And that was that. Wasn't anything at all anyone could do to help her. So the fathers would just keep all of them inside after a while. They wouldn't even let them go to the market.

The flip side of the coin is the hard core extremists. They're everywhere. In Afghanistan, these guys were the ones walking around beating the people if they didn't go pray and shooting people in the back of the head. That was until we went there. They were also hiding Osama. That started the whole thing. There was this one time...

We were making house to house searches because we had gotten intel about Al-Qaeda in the neighborhood. Supposedly, this guy had blown up a convoy a couple of days earlier. We made several stops and then got to this one house. I was the second one in. When we got to the door, we heard screaming from inside like a little kid or something. We busted in and there was friggin raggie sodomizing this little boy. Anyway, he turned and grabbed for his gun. He was shot dead right then and there. Case over. I'd heard a lot of crap about that kind of stuff but I saw this one with my own two eyes. I guess it's pretty common. Actually, some of them claim those little boys as a trophy. I think it's their dirty little secret. That son-of-a-bitch deserved what he got-even if he weren't Al-Qaeda. But he was.

Chapter 6
Teddy

He brushed her hair back a little and kissed her on the cheek.

"Teddy, I never thought this day would come. I am sooo happy!"

He reached over and rubbed her big tummy, and then said in a broken voice, "Neither did I, my little pregnant girl."

Her eyes lit up again and he just let her go...he knew her plans would dominate the next ten minutes of conversation.

"I want to do the baby's room all blue. And then I want to get an intercom system..."

His girl had become a woman now. She was that Midwestern all American girl that Carrie Underwood sang about. His girl. His wife. And soon-to-be mother of his children. He was a happy, happy man.

He interrupted her with a kiss and pulled her face

toward his. She kept rattling on til he just took a kiss on her moist red lips. She glowed.

"Careful now, that's what got me in this condition."

* * *

Time passed and she delivered a healthy boy, and he was strong just like his daddy. Teddy was a good father too. He raised him right and popped his little hand if he didn't listen. The boy knew right from wrong. He would help his mother set the table and watch his father work on the car. He could get a wrench or a can of oil and even feed the cat. Mom and dad had sown seeds of prosperity that the boy would carry all his life. He had learned the two most important things: God has a plan for him and a man has to work.

Then Teddy was called to active duty.

Sadness loomed in the air.

"Son, daddy has to go away now so you will be the man around here."

Teddy stood there looking up at his daddy.

"Where goin', daddy?"

Teddy choked on his words and faltered a minute.

"I have to go away and get some bad guys. They came here and killed a lotta people."

Teddy remembered his daddy used to say "fue bye bye" when he was learning Spanish in college. And he knew that meant "gone away."

✻   ✻   ✻

The boy looked down and a tear shot out of both eyes and made lines down his face. Teddy bent down and picked him up. He kissed him on his face and a tear brimmed on each of his own eyes. Amanda stood there shaking silently with a red face. She grabbed him and they all hugged. Teddy's tears overflowed and the dam broke.

In the background, the news reported..."Senator Kennedy told reporters that he would fight incessantly for the right to same sex unions...Christian groups vowed to oppose any legislation...."

Teddy breathed in Amanda's perfume and the innocence of his boy for a few seconds more and pulled free, very, very gently and began to pray,.

"Dear Heavenly Father, in the name of Jesus, we come to You and thank you for the blessings You have bestowed on us. We humbly submit to the work and the plans You have for us. I ask You to watch over Amanda and David in the name of Jesus, to protect them and to comfort them. Please lead them and be their refuge..."

Amanda broke in, "and protect Daddy, in the name of Jesus, we pray and give him to Your hands in the name of Jesus, Amen."

Six months later.

The sun was setting and most of the people in the neighborhood had made it home and started supper. The black family a couple of doors over were wondering the whereabouts of their eldest. A block or two over, Charles slinked in his sofa with his nightly tirade.

"Goddamnit! Those damn Republicans ! I hate those motherfuckers! And they always fuckin try to stop someone from getting something. You know, I don't even know why I fuckin pay taxes."

He took another big gulp of whisky and coke. He drank nightly til he was blind-*er*. And he hated God.

In some other city, a future presidential contender whose heart was as black as his skin was in a church pew listening to a heretic. An old black man. A hate monger.

"...and God damn America for what it's done to the black man..." His congregation clapped and profaned the name of the Lord with an 'Amen.' And they were ignorant. So they lived and so they died-in darkness. And they never prospered. They didn't know that faith works by love.

Such are those that give in to false doctrine for the price of a few dollars. They have traded their souls and their heritage for a bowl of porridge. Jacob I loved but Esau I hated.

✯ ✯ ✯

In Baltimore, a young black soldier was leaving his night class at the university. He had tuition reimbursed by the military. His little brother had taken out government loans and was attending another college upstate. They both were making full use of the opportunities afforded every single American citizen to improve their lives without regard to color, religion or anything else-even ex-convicts could do the same. The soldier was in a hurry to get home. He had duty that next morning.

✯ ✯ ✯

A block over from the soldier, two black men watched the street for anyone who might fall prey. They had never worked a day in their lives...and never would. They were beasts in the street.

Time passed.

Amanda had just arrived from her class, with David in tow and groceries in hand. The phone rang. She picked it up with one hand and groceries in the other. David looked at her as she listened.

She broke down and started to sob. She whispered into the phone and then hung up.

"Thank you for calling."

She paused a minute and wiped her eye. Then she turned and put down the groceries.

"Come here, son. Mommy needs to tell you something."

And they cried together.

David was indeed the man of the house for a long, long time to come. And people around the world lived in freedom because of the sacrifice of that family. An Afghani boy whose mother was killed because she hid her boy from being sodomized later went to be a governor in his province. A girl whose father was shot in head because the local extremists saw him playing soccer in shorts went to the American University of Afghanistan. A shepherd boy whose brother was gutted and whose head was hung on a post after his discovery of a poppy field later went to college in the city. He lived a peaceful life.

Across the street, a Democrat complained because her check had too much taxes taken out. In Denver, a terrorist suspect was intercepted en route to his next destination. He had C-4 explosives in his possession. An Al-Qaeda had given that information during an interrogation after a raid in Ramalli. In Yemen a drone intelligence aircraft surveyed a band of heavily armed Al Qaeda near Jizan. Information leading to their whereabouts had also been obtained in Iraq after a raid in Erbil. Two American soldiers had been killed in that operation. The unit secured 3600 rounds of ammunition, 160 grenades, 4 mortars, and took 8 terrorists were taken into custody. This was only after 8 hours of heavy fighting. 16 Al Qaeda had also been killed. Also discovered was an elaborate torture chamber. Sixteen bodies had been placed in a shallow grave immediately outside the underground shaft where the discoveries had been made.

And a mexican in Houston attached a mexican flag on his $24,000 SUV that he had gotten only after securing employment in the US. He was on a work visa for WalMart. He had been in the states for a year. His wife was 9 months pregnant. They had big plans. Neither could speak English. Neither one had any desire to learn. He illegally carried a concealed weapon. He hated the American people although nobody knew him. His little brother and uncle had snuck over the border and stayed with him. The little brother sold drugs. He could speak English.

❋   ❋   ❋

Just south of the University of Houston in a bad neighborhood, three brothas were talking. Jamal claimed he **had to** sell drugs .

"Yo man!" He waved his hand with his fingers cocked crooked. "I gotsta sell me some stuff cuz aint no white motherfucker gonna give a brotha a job! I aint workin for no ten fuckin' dollars an hour either."

His mother opened the back door and yelled, "Jamal, that man called you again today!"

She stood there and looked at them. Two dolla (as

they called him because he always said" "let me get two dolla from ya.") lowered the joint and looked at Jamal whispering, "Yo, man, I thought you said she don't come out here."

"Relax, man" Jamal whispered back sideways out of his mouth.

"Yo, mama, Im gonna call him," Jamal shouted back.

Mikie lowered his bottle of Thunderbird. Best wine on the market for the price. It had the kick of a mule in about five minutes.

The screen slammed shut with a bit of disgust in the motion.

"Damn! I wish she'd get off my ass bout gettin' a damn job."

"Hey yo man, you need to call him. I'll take it if you don't," said Mikie.

"Nigga please. Aint no friggin peckerwood gonna give you shit! You gonna go down there and be his damn Tom. That's what he wants."

"Daaaamn, why in the fuck u put in a application then?" Mikie said.

"Pass that fuckin blunt, nigga." Jamal inhaled the smoke and held it as long as he could, then blew out as he talked. "Jes ta get her off my ass!"

They all laughed.

His mother had four children by three different fathers. Never did marry. Never was asked. She had gotten pregnant at 16. They lived in one of the worst areas in the city. She worked one legitimate job in her life. Now at 56, she cleaned houses and collected food stamps. She had voted only once but ran her mouth constantly about the way the country was run. She had no idea where Iraq was, what partial-birth abortion was, or what went on past her little neighborhood. All she could see was what stood directly in front of her. Two of her sons had been in prison. Her only daughter had also gotten pregnant at 16 and now had two children. All of them lived together. The daughter, now 21, had had her own house on section 8 low rent housing from the government. But her ex-boyfriend had beaten her up several times for having different men back and forth so she let it go and moved back home with her mother. She also was unemployed. She had always been unemployed. She was on welfare.

"Hey Jamal, why don't you go in the army like lil Tony? He's makin' cash money!"

"Naw, Mikie, what the fuckin government ever done for me? Aint no mothufucka gave me shit!" He spit on the ground for emphasis.

Two dolla jumped in, "Hey Nigga, Lil Tony got it goin on. He gotta fine ole lady. He gotta nice crib. He pushin a nice ride."

"Motherfuck him! He's a pussy ass. I make my OWN money."

And he did. Day in and day out, he walked the street selling rocks. Strapped all the time.

He continued, "...I dont want nobody tellin me what to do. What I look like? Like I'm 15 or somethin? Besides I got this fuckin case on me."

"That dont mean nuthin," Two dolla said. "You'll jes hafta go to boot camp or some shit. You can go and get pumped up. That's it. They dont wanna keep a nigga for first time."

Inside the house, his sister was cooking. The smell was a magnet and in a minute three cockroaches appeared on the table in the living room where the kids were eating. The four year old boy saw the biggest roach-a big fat one with a tail of 700 eggs inside. It crawled near his plate and he simply made a gesture to scare it away. It left and then came back. A smaller roach crawled on the edge of the one year old's plate and started feasting. Its antennae waved back and forth in delight. When Jamal was a young boy, he used to shoot them with rubber bands. Now he didn't think about them at all.

The bugle blew and Amanda and David stood motionless as the soldiers performed their salute. They were surrounded by love and honor. Before them lay their duty. The blare of the trumpet cut the air until every note gathered together just over the burial site. There the sound formed an umbrella. The notes went up and down. almost lulling, and then rose slowly, just above the crowd and then sank down around each individual there, caressing them softly, and comforting their last minute with Teddy. Amanda was dressed in black and David wore his blue church suit Teddy had picked out shortly before deployment. That was for Christmas Sunday. He had grown into it.

The music stopped and then silence. The ceremony continued. David saw the soldiers salute and lifted his hand to his head and saluted, too. He knew what it meant.

Before deployment...

Teddy leaned over and wiped the tear from her eye. "If I go, don't look at that box there because I won't be in there." He reached over and pointed to her chest and then touched her over her heart, ever so gently. "I'll be here...and there." He pointed up. "To be absent from the body is to be with Jesus." He smiled and she lay her head down in his lap. They loved each other more than the whole wide world.

Chapter 7
Justified

January 2007
American University of Kuwait

"I'm not voting for Tareq because he seems like he's always thinking about bossing people around or something," said Miryam.

"Excuse me, girl, that's what the class president does!" said Amena. "Besides, I think he's cute."

The three girls laughed and Razia chimed in.

"Look, this is the first election we have had so we have to vote and be heard..OK?"

They all agreed and went on with their studies. Miryam remembered a conversation she had had with her mother just a couple of weeks before. This was democracy in action. It was a very new thing for the women of Kuwait, and what better place for one to be immersed in it than the American University--of Kuwait. It had been a turbulent time. Blood had been the watering source for this garden of freedom-American blood. Now women could vote. Now hardliners weren't the only ones in power. Now women had the freedom to drive. Now women could choose their own destiny-although they still couldn't choose who they wanted to marry. But progress was inching along. Miryam was just seven years old at the time but she still remembered...

August 1991

Somewhere in Kuwait City...

The mother huddled around her children as the armed intruders wearing Iraqi uniforms ransacked the house. They were hungry and looking for anything to sate their appetites. They roamed through the apartment sniffing around and uncovering everything. Like a pack of wolves that had cornered its prey, they secured the area and searched every nook and cranny of the spacious apartment. This was the richer area of the city. The husband wrestled with one of the men. But he was fat and out of shape. He became winded after just a half a minute and the soldier hit him in the stomach with the butt of his rifle. The father bent over, fell to his knees, and gasped for air.

The other men fanned out and went through each room, throwing out every drawer and sifting the contents. They picked up anything that shined in the hope it was worth something. Across the alley, another group of soldiers did the same. There they found a mother, her daughter and an uncle. The uncle was a younger man, mid thirties, slender, a soccer enthusiast. The numbers had been meticulously stripped from each building with the knowledge that the soldiers would come looking for the leaders of the community. This would hopefully throw them off the trail of money and power.

The government offices had been raided the day before and the word spread quickly across the Kuwaiti community. Many had fled.

In Washington, D.C., a Democrat senator was in a press conference. He was the same coward a he had been as a child, but now he wore a suit and tie.

"This is not our fight. The Republican party has an ulterior motive here, and Mr. President, the American people are putting you on notice: We will not let our men and women of our great United States go to this foreign land simply so you, Mr. President, can take over their country just the same as the Iraqis and rob them of their oil."

Meanwhile...President Bush was in a meeting looking over the intelligence collected on Kuwaiti casualties. Loads of people had been taken away and no intelligence was to be had on them, and so it would remain forever.

Across the alley, the two soldiers who remained to 'guard' the house raided the refrigerator. A 15 year old girl came from the back with her hair in a fluff and in her nightgown. The two looked at each other and grinned.

The uncle ran at them and the mother started screaming as the small boy watched. He urinated on himself. The two men attacked the uncle and beat him severely. He fought with every ounce but every time he would get to his knees, they would stomp him back down. One of the soldiers laughed and hit him in the head five or six times with the butt of the rifle. He crumpled back to the floor motionless but still breathing.

One of the men grabbed the mother and the other grabbed the girl. The girl was dragged back into the bedroom and raped violently. This was her first time and blood was everywhere. She screamed but he put a pillow over her face. The other soldier grabbed the mother by the hair and shoved her to her knees as the boy watched. She cried and screamed and then collected herself...

"Please...please..my son..please..no.. not in front of him."

He wrenched her head tighter and looked behind him and opened the door of the closet and kicked the boy inside. He made her do things as the uncle lay bleeding and semi-unconscious.

One hour later...

The uncle was dragged outside of the house and into the main street of the neighborhood. The people from the block were gathered ...perhaps twenty or thirty to witness.

The uncle was forced to kneel. The mother and daughter screamed and pleaded and cried and it all fed the greedy ears of the soldiers. Other soldiers in the area had gathered, as well.

A rapist spoke, "For willfully fighting against the peaceful annexation, the sentence of death has been pronounced to avoid further bloodshed."

The uncle tried to stand but was held at the shoulders on each side. The two soldiers on each side stood back and the rapist shot him in the back of the head.

In Washington, the democrats continued to decry American involvement.

"...we are not the police of the world...and American soil is not at stake. We are the most powerful government in the history of the world. There has never been an attack on American soil in Modern America and there never will be...."

There is always a time when evil will be repaid upon a country, just like it is repaid on a man. Some call it fate. Some call it karma. Some call it poetic justice. Whatever the answer, it comes back. The same ones who had raped their maids from the poorest countries in the world-the Philippines, Indonesia, Sri Lanka-were witnessing these same atrocities on their own flesh and blood. Their women and sons alike were violated. As an evil is so possessed, so it refuses to change. Even today, these domestics are held in servitude, legal slavery. After completion of their contracts, they still cannot leave the country without the permission from their sponsor. They have no recourse but to run when raped. Then they are charged with absconding and if caught thrown in jail indefinitely. This is the law. And so it remains even as you read.

And they huddled in the midst of occupation. And they cried again and again: "George Bush, come! Come!"

They were reduced to an animalistic existence. With no income, the poor sold and bartered all that they had for bread. Water was the most precious. And the houses stunk and the people stunk. And the haughty spirit departed. The maids and the upper crust were huddled alike. And they cried together.

And the weeks moved like sludge. Their riches were useless but to buy a little more. The jewelry was gone. The fine clothes. It was all gone. Traded for water or bread or stolen by the Iraqis. The people languished except for the glimmer of hope that their friend-the United States of America-would come. And the destiny of the man is always tested amidst the scoffing of cowardice. The forces were mobilized, and they came. Their day of liberation was here. There was dancing in the streets. Hundreds had been carried off and were never heard from again-men, women, and children. Even more murdered-in front of their families. Countless raped in front of their brothers and fathers and mothers. Over time, and with help from their friends, the Kuwaiti people put their shattered pieces back together, and they began to prosper once more. And the money rolled in. All was well once again. But the laws never changed and again some maids are crying out, "Come!" But no one hears. Raped, beaten, starved, and never paid, they still cry at this very moment. Evil always dares the just, and some people never learn. BUT TO WHOM MUCH IS GIVEN, MUCH IS REQUIRED.

Chapter 8
Bondage

Friday afternoon and the family had packed the living room. The women were bustling about the kitchen, running between the tables and the pots, moving this and reheating that. The children sat at their assigned places anxiously awaiting the weekly feast. The grandfather listened to a story from one of his sons. 67 people had gathered again and each had his special tale of triumph to impart. The opulent setting glimmered in the afternoon sunshine that flowed like waves from the open curtains. The expensive furniture had been moved back to accommodate the massive gathering. BMWs, a Mercedes, and a jaguar were parked in front and several escalades were situated along the street in front of the tiny palace. A guard strolled the grounds-an Indian in a uniform. A Filipina maid listened intently to the barking of one of the women.

Miryam helped in the kitchen and did as she was

instructed by the elder females. Two of her uncles had been murdered in the invasion years earlier. As the society would have it, their widows were damaged goods and never remarried. They did, however, sneak. A retarded boy stood at the stove picking at the food. He pulled over a pot and spilled some rice on the floor. The maid quickly bent down and wiped it up. An aunt yelled at the maid. The children ran screaming through the halls creating havoc as they went. They went unchecked-everywhere. The maids hated these days.

Miryam stared at her distant cousin as he laughed and jumped in glee at his mess on the floor. His mother and father were cousins too. She had a boyfriend, secretly. She was a good girl, an unpicked flower, a dutiful daughter. She loved the boy but he was from a different family. They could never be married. It was forbidden. To do so would taint the blood.

She had wrestled with that for years. She had been raised to think for herself but also to do as she was told. She was told that she was equal. She was important. She was the elite in society. She was made to accomplish something in life and help people, Then again, the Filipino driver was poor because God hated them. They were inferior. The Indian house boy was filthy-and he was. He stank. All other cultures were whores-mostly anyway. Like her pets, she had to care for them and feed them and make sure they had sufficient shelter but they were still unclean. They were there to serve and serve only. They did serve too-willingly or un-. In addition to all of that, she never could reconcile her position in all of that. In fact, her father was so "fair" that he wouldn't even accept a dowry for her. To do that would mean that he needed the money, and he didn't. After all, he was extremely wealthy. They were lucky to marry his daughter. She remembered he had told her once that in India, people were in a caste that they could never get out of...unlike her, she had been born into a free society and she could form her own world. That was her heritage in the new Kuwait.

But she never could understand how a man had the right to tell his daughter who could stick his thing inside of her all the days of her life-til death. If she was elite...If she had the right to choose her own way...if she were indeed one of the chosen ones on earth...if she had been made for something...how could someone else tell her that she had to let someone she never wanted to crawl on top of her and slobber on her and put his big fat nasty belly on her and breathe on her with his cigarette breath and grunt a couple of times on her and in her ear like her friend said her husband did and then roll over and fall to sleep? ...she wasn't a toilet....

No, not my daddy she thought. He would never ever in a million years do that. He loves me. I am his girl.

Her father was a fat man. He carried his girth as a sign of success. He wore custom made thobes for $1000

USD. He drove the finest cars all selected in accordance with his mood. Educated in America, and with the an Ivy League degree, he had commanded his way in life, mostly bought though. He had never really worked, only if taking tea and meeting over dinners was to be considered real work,. Yet he was elite. His family had money and power. He too had married "within the family." It was hard though to distinguish where the family started and began, except in the case of marrying first cousins...which was considered ideal in this culture. In other cases, only a gamble of the genes would determine who had had relations with whom and only that could be decidedly confirmed at birth. Many times, the interlocking cousins would be the children of a third or fourth wife who had been the first cousin of this one and/or that one. It was a circle. The class in society was determined by family name and just as justice was meted and doled out according to name, so was one's spouse. This glutton had everyTHING. But he had no soul.

There was no righteousness in him. Miryam loved her father. She was a daddy's girl and she was very weak because of it. She too had never worked a day in her life. Her job was school. Work was for the poor. The menial job was for the menial heritage. She was born for something else. And that was her life. She felt sorry for her friends because all of them had at one time or another fallen in love but were unable to marry because they too were relegated to the family's gene pool. And the boy never chose. It was always the decision of the parents. Then the mother would consult her circle as would the father. After a suitable match was found, the two were thrown together for a meeting to see if they were compatible. One could accept or reject the other...but only at an angle of repose. Rarely would there be a second meeting. Like show dogs, they would or they would not.

The decisions were made as alliances for business and power. Deals were made and the barter system was in full force. Many a tacit agreement was formed over a cup of tea. The decisions were made by the patriarch because the children were his property... each assigned according to birth and justified according to the dictate of the patriarch. No one was equal to them but their class. All else were made to serve them. Each individual was cast into his caste. One could never cross over.

The family had finished and gathered in many small circles in the giant living room. Miryam's father clinked a fork on a glass and looked solemnly for the crowd to become quiet. This was all about him.

"I want to announce that Miryam has accepted a proposal to Khaled. Mabrook. We look forward to their prosperous union. May Allah bless their family and all that they do. Mabrook!"

The family turned and stared at her and cheers broke out.

She awoke to her name. Her thinking became clear. Her heart sank and she felt the tentacles of slavery circle around her. She labored to breathe... and she became another head of cattle...in a beautiful chrome palace.

She was paired to breed.

This was her only notice.

Chapter 9
Bryce

Bryce was a good man. He had been a good boy all his life. He humbled himself before the Lord and God spoke to him and led him. And He protected him. And he was safe. He began to praise the Lord quietly, and even then the Lord spoke to him. And his praise welled up inside of him again and again. A man who has never humbled himself can never understand that. Not that he was special but he was different. He had a special understanding. He still experienced tough times. So he had to stop for refueling just like a man stops for a day with a close friend—a time to get away and get advice. He would get up early and study and pray simply to spend time with the Lord. Like a champion who gets up and trains while the world is still sleeping so he did. Sometimes he wished it could stay 4 am all day long. It was sweet and it made him whole. He was an educated man. His spirit was godly. His hands were trained for war. He was humble. And he was in service to the king of heaven and earth.

Bryce's brother Duran was a humble man too. But he had had his wild time. Yet those days were just a whisper in the tornado of life. Now he too was grounded on bedrock. He also had a knowledge that took him into the secret place, as Mike Murdock called it. Sharing the same father and mother, thoroughly bred through and through, they were blood. They were of the same physical and spiritual family. They were of one body and one mind. He had married a colored girl. Mixed with black American and Cajun descent, she bore him a son. Rory was his name. And the line was strong. The father's grandfather had passed on the tradition of service to his son and so it rolled. But the beginnings of the knowledge and relationship to God were born from fear. Over time and through the lineage, the understanding sharpened and a clarity evolved. This was a relationship of love and dedication. It started with the sacrifice of the King. And the family understood that. Bryce and Duran's father had also had a wild stretch. But they returned to what they had been taught. They all knew to teach a boy in the way and he won't depart from it.

But there is a time when a man gives himself over. He gives his spirit and it's a willing sacrifice. He learns after that initial gift that sacrifice is continuous. It cannot be given and then taken back. It's just like forgiveness. If it is taken back, the end is worse than the beginning. It is like a general in service to his country who then says bad things about the commander-in-chief. He is black inside-or outside. He is not a real man and never could be. He is an embarrassment. The sons learned these things from their father. Their father had been a fighter and a wrestler. Duran was a champion wrestler and Bryce was a champion boxer. The grandfather had also been a boxer. And so the art of physical and spiritual combat was passed on. It was a rite of passage and a way of life.

Through the line, the women played their part. But no one can teach a man to be man but a man. Through the years, they learned the heart of David-humility, service, education, control, and sacrifice. It was their father who taught them these things. They had seen him train as a fighter. They had seen him open his Bible and talk openly to his king. They learned through his weakness and also through his strength. He was just a man and they knew it-prone to mistakes in his man-ness and just as willing to say "I am sorry." He taught them and showed them their responsibility in life. They knew who they were as a result. The test of their manhood though never came through the ring. It came through standing on their biblical teachings. They learned to apply it. They learned through their time in the Middle East as children who they actually were. They knew that they were children of promise, heirs, from the seed of Isaac and Jacob. They claimed healing and saw it. As youngsters in public and private school, they also knew the difference between the magnanimity of real equality and lip service.

They knew the falsity of career Christians versus a real relationship. Such a contrast was in their private school where their father taught after returning from three years in Saudi Arabia. They went to school at a private school in Dallas, Texas. Here they understood what public consumption actually was. They saw it in the church that stood on the hill overlooking Northwest Highway. It stood as a beacon there. But there was a legalistic oppressive spirit at work,. The pastor there was what their father called a "career Christian." That was how he made his living. Boasting being called into ministry at the age of seven, the pastor laughed with the fasle cackle of a male Fran Dresher. It was programmed to respond automatically.

The deceptive legalism of the pastor Headley and his twisting of the believers' trust was evident one Sunday morning when he forced new believers to repeat after him-this before the congregation of several hundred people. They promised to come faithfully to that church only and also bring their tithes to that specific church-only. As offensive and heretical as it was, the father used it to teach his boys, and he separated from the church almost immediately. This was the career Christian at work, twisting the Word of God, misleading the people, and bringing the mission of the church into ill repute. The long shadow of the Lighthouse on the hill was tainted by he to whom it had been entrusted.

But this was then and is not the things that go on. They always have and they always will. Bryce knew that. He and Duran were never allowed to let seeds of doubt take root. Their father took his place as priest of the home. He always made sure to use an opportunity to teach. Their father was no saint though. But they learned. Like with people who really do know the truth, when they strayed away, they always came back. Liberty is no occasion to sin, but things do happen, especially when we don't pay mind to the things that we should. A stray glance here or a sideways wink there, it's a slippery slope. So diligence was the key.

And Bryce knew that. He made it his habit to study daily and talk with his Creator. As he grew older, he grew stronger. His strength was from the inside out. He had a peace that no one around him could understand. He didn't panic and he always found an answer. His belief justified him and that led him to peace. His hope and his faith was the anchor of his soul. Compared to many who have a faint glimmer of understanding, he actually knew that he knew. This set him apart. There was no speculation on his part and his Word counseled him daily. Bryce spent time in the Word and this was the daily cleansing, the reassurance, the washing that rejuvenated him. It was his power, his salvation, and his success. No matter what happened around him, he knew everything would be ok. He saw it a million times before. He lived it and breathed it. It was part of him and he was part of it. It was bigger than him but it had all been done for him. That was the dichotomy. That was the overwhelming aspect of his whole belief system. His Creator had come and paid the price for simple Bryce's iniquity, and his name had been known by God from the foundation of time. From his very first encounter with Jesus, God incarnate-God manifest in the flesh-he couldn't walk away. Although he stumbled and although he fell, he always got up and got right back on track. That grace in which he lived was never an occasion to sin but always an occasion to become once again in the steadfastness of his destiny, the destiny to which he had been called form the beginning of time and that which every single human that has ever walked the planet has had the opportunity to experience-even before the law was written and countermanded by the new law of faith...even then, the law of right and wrong had been written on the tablet of one's heart.

So at every stumbling, he came back and asked for forgiveness because he also knew where his sin had abounded, grace abounded even further. So he lived accordingly.

But as one who would never rewrite his theology in the face of peril or under attack, he waxed stronger and became a real warrior. The battles never stop coming so learned how to engage conflict. The success he lived both spiritually and materially were bought and paid for with a price. The blood of Jesus stands as the prototype of the blood of Bryce's comrades in arms-through that blood freedom was obtained and it's a continual bloodshed...a continual fight. Unlike the blood shed here in war, the prototype was one that was sacrificed once and for all.

But the battle against evil here on earth requires diligence.

It IS a constant battle.

With this knowledge sanctified or set apart in his heart, no matter what he saw, no matter what he felt, no matter what appeared to be the truth, Brycie knew that no weapon formed against him would prosper. In this he found rest. In this he found strength. In this he found victory-every single time. He knew that what he knew superseded what his senses told him.

And through time, he rejoiced ion every single circumstance. He didn't rejoice BECAUSE he was getting shot at. He rejoiced throughout the experience, knowing that it would produce endurance, and it did. That endurance produced character and made him the man he was. In turn that character produced more hope in him. The hope an anchor to his soul. It held him and uplifted him at the perfect time. It made him even stronger. He was never ever disappointed. This was his heritage and the heritage of all who believed like him, as well.

✷   ✷   ✷

This was an American family. It had the mix. It was mixed. But it doesn't have to be. It can be all white or all black or all brown. America's history and present was and is a choice. Every person chose his own way. They married whomever they pleased, and it worked. Bryce had a Hispanic girl, a white father, and a black mother. Her grandmother was Indian. Duran's wife was black and Cajun. Duran and Bryce's great great grandfather on the mother's side was German, and on the father's side, the great-great-great grandfather was French. He had come to America to help civilize the West.

These were real Americans. Some folks errantly refer to these as "mutt" because of the racial mixture. A "mutt" is a mutt of the spirit. Either you are an American or you're not. America is NOT a nation of immigrants. *It is a nation of Americans*. It is not an immigrant culture but the American culture. There is no such place as Africa America. You can't be Mexican and American. Either you're American or you're not. You can't be both at the same time. There is no in-between. Every person has a past but the present always overtakes the past-it has already overtaken the past. And the future is determined by the present. America doesn't want more immigrants. America wants more Americans. We're not a country to be raped but to be cultivated. A piece of fabric that is grafted into a nice sofa becomes part of that sofa. It is no longer distinct but serves the purpose of the aggregate. And the creator will meticulously choose that piece of fabric so that it will blend into and become part of the sofa. Without the nice sofa, the fabric, simply that-fabric...in and of itself, is useless. The less is blessed by the better. We are distinct and separate, and, above and beyond all, we are the here and now that creates the universal American-**ness** that will go forth into the future as it has in the past to be described in one word and one word only: American.

America means liberty and choice but within the confines of decorum, morality, and legality. People do have the right to choose their own destiny.

And their freedom to choose should never be an occasion to sin, nor an occasion to kill. It's the opportunity to build and grow. And right and wrong has never been predicated on the possibility that one would kill. The other choices are free but liberty is never an occasion to sin. Liberty is NOT adultery. Liberty is NOT abortion. Liberty is NOT perversions. But a distinction must be made. The law has no marriage to adultery and perversion between consenting adults. Abortion IS a legal thing: the legality of murder. And the same that commit that usually commit adultery and perversions. But adultery and perversions sin against one's own body and against one's spouse. The spouse can leave. Abortion sins against the innocent child. There is no recourse against that-no fix.

Killing a an unborn child during a crime is now legally defined as murder....

But, proponents say, "The woman will have it done anyway and may die if we don't legalize it!"

Since when do we may the greater wrong available on the POSSIBILITY that one will knowingly commit suicide through murder?

But, proponents say, "Even an animal will gnaw off its foot to get out of a trap!"

A baby is NOT a foot.

And these are pagans...what pagans sacrifice, they offer to demons and not to God.

These are the mutts of the spirit for they want to drink of the cup of the Lord and the cup of demons. One can't partake of the table of the Lord and the table of demons. Shall we provoke the Lord to jealousy? Are we stronger that He?

To accept all with open arms is a perversion of the spirit and it defiles the covering that we established over ourselves at the beginning. It festers and it invites incursions. It led to the fall of the Roman Empire, and it led to 911. It's a spiritual adultery.

✻   ✻   ✻

The Arrogant American

There is a thing about silence. It can make a fool seem wise or a wise man seem a fool. It just depends on who is doing the looking. Saturday night as it went and most of the men were out for the night. This was pre-deployment. Everyone knew what lay ahead and they were getting ready. For some, that meant making their few final calls, and for others that meant tying one on. They were in a no man's land here-every man's land-every nationality under the sun was here. It was a hot spot for those who had little sense and no vision for the future. These were the men who said "Let us eat and drink for tomorrow we die."

The others who were not there had already died to the baser things in life. They had already sacrificed themselves to the higher calling and knew of the new tomorrow./ But these were the ones although fighting for the freedom of people they would never know still had no knowledge themselves. They weren't given over like the beasts they were going to fight but neither had they given themselves over to the spiritual understanding of who they were and who they could become. They lived in ignorance.

Bryce made his way through the street teeming with people. It was the weekend and they were drinking. These were soldiers sent from their respective countries to stabilize

Iraq. So they drank because they knew they might not see the next 48 hours. They were the minority. Three men sat at a table outside a bar. They were drinking heavily and they were loud. Bryce was alone and he had picked up just a few items and was returning to the base.

One of the men called to Bryce who was out of uniform. "Hey American!" He had a thick accent.

Bryce looked at him and nodded but kept walking. As he approached their direction he heard a low comment and then they started laughing.

"Hey Kaffir!"

Bryce knew what it meant. He kept walking.

"You fucking Americans. You always think you're so damn superior!"

The foreigner threw a bottle at Bryce. Bryce stopped, and looked at them. The three laughed again.

"Hey Kaffir, what's wrong with you? You dropped something." The foreigner got up and walked into the street.

Bryce could hear his father, "Ya aint got nothin to prove but you always got an area of an arm's length. That's your attack zone."

"Fucking Americans...like a bunch of fucking dogs.

You always gotta start some shit!" He reached out to push Bryce.

Bryce ducked under and slid inside with two double left hooks to the body. The drunk crumpled. Bryce walked away and went on about his business.

Chapter 10
Amalgamation

At the base, 7:45 PM
In the billiards room

Several soldiers are sitting talking over a beer
An Hispanic nicknamed "Mexico", a country boy called "Arkansas", Bryce, and a black man -"Northeast"

Arkansas, "Look man, we hadda go in there cuz he was even fuckin killin his own people. In fact, even after we kicked his ass outta Kuwait, he continued to defy the Security Council's resolutions."

Brycie, "It's true. He had stuff to make weapons anyweay. Any friggin' way it goes, he COULD make weapons."

Mexico, " Did they actually find anything at all?"

B: "Yeah man, they found chemicals. Even mustard gas is classified as a weapon of mass destruction. What more proof does the world need? That's officially why they executed his ass-he gassed 4000 of his own people-men, women, and children. "

M: "I didn't know that."

A: "Yeah, that's cuz y'all aint got no TVs in Mexico, huh?" (laughs-jokingly)

M: "I'm not Mexican. I'm American." (emphasis added)

A: "I know. I know. I'm just jokin' with you, buddy."

Mexico smiles.

NE:" He had weapons for sure. Just cuz they didn't find actual nuclear bombs doesn't mean he wasn't workin' on 'em. In fact, why in the hell wouldn't he let weapons inspectors in there? For months, the weapons inspectors were turned away. That's like some chick coming over and her boyfriend won't let her in the house. Hell, he's got another woman in there!"

They all laugh.

A: "You know all about that, dontcha, Northeast?" (ribbing him)

NE: "Naw, man. I got one lady and one lady only. That's enough for me."

B: "I hear ya. Me too. One is all I got time for and besides, who needs a dozen hamburgers when you got steak at home?"

They all laugh again. The mood is light and they all agree on the war. Today was good.

M: "Yeah but what about all those people getting'

killed? I mean, everyone says that if we never came here, then they wouldn't be dying...."

B: "Actually, that's proof that we NEED to be here. The people getting' killed are getting' killed by the terrorists themselves. Look at it like this, The people fighting us were here under Saddam's regime and went unfettered. They could come and go freely, to and from Syria, some over the Iranian border, especially in the mountainous regions. So when we overthrew Saddam, they didn't just fight us. Man they started blowing up buses, schools, markets, killing men, women, and children. Man they are killing kids man! Kids !!!"

M: "Yeah, I know all that but if we DIDN'T come here, then what?"

B: "Then Saddam would have remained in power. He would have acquired nuclear weapons. The people that are killing innocent civilians would have gotten stronger and stronger. With the intricate network that they have set up around the world, especially with modern technology and internet and all that crap, we would have had another 911 somewhere down the line. To me, it's basically this simple: the fact that they are killing innocent civilians, the people they have lived next to all their lives is proof enough that we are in the right to be here. Because if they kill their own friggin' neighbors, they will be knockin' on our doorstep again. In fact, with all this open immigration crap, we let 'em in and they are still there."

Mexico is perturbed a little at the immigration remark.

M: "Wait a minute! You mean you're against immigration?"

B: "Nope! It's just that we need to stick to our guns a lil and let in the people who can contribute to our economy."

NE: "Yeah that's true."

A: "Amen!"

M: "Damn! You are some racist SOBs!"

B: "That ain't true. Look, we let in all those Lebanese after the civil war in Beirut and millions of Palestinians too. They flocked to Michigan and even now they do, as well, under the guise of going to school. That's now considered a radical hotbed for Islamists. Not that Islam is bad per se but the nuts who wanna kill us and eat our bread at the same time...well...you decide."

He hit a chord with Arkansas.

A: "Yeah, that's right." (raising his voice) " Crap, if they gonna come here-ANYBODY- they need to assimilate!"

M: "That's a pretty big word, country boy!" (He's angry)

A: "Yeah, well you know what" It's called English, my friend" (He gets up in Mexico's face on the last word.

M: "You need to sit your ass back, country boy before I teach you a lesson."

A: "Anytime, anywhere...I don't even need an invitation. Just say the word." (Bowed up and ready to fight)

Arkansas would have whipped him like a bad dog. They all knew it.

B: "Ok, calm down, both of you. Anyway, the fact that these idiots are blowing up their own neighbors proves that we are in the right. If a cop sees a man robbing an elderly couple will he not jump in to help? And if the old lady gets killed because there is an ensuing gunbattle, does that mean the cop was wrong to get involved?" he waits a couple of seconds for an answer. "Hell no!"

M: "Ok. Ok. You got a point. But America is still made up of immigrants. We can't jsut close the doors."

NE: "Ok, Mexico, answer me this. Does Mexico hire outside labor to come in and do factory work in, say, Mexico City?"

M: "No, of course not. We do our own work."

NE: "That's right, and so do we. We have a work ethic that says every man has to get out and make his own way. These countries that don't do that now have a huge unemployment problem. They got that cradle to grave mentality and the young guys live at home until they are 30 or OLDER. Most of them have no job. No work ethic. No physical stamina even. They whine and point fingers at the government and then blame their own government because they can't get work. In Saudi Arabia, that led to insurrection against their own government. In France, it caused rioting in the streets with the second generation immigrants. They were setting stuff on fire and everything else. They EXPECT to be handed something. They holed up and created their own little ghettos. It's true in England and even in Amsterdam too. In fact, England has really drawn the line on immigrants coming in by imposing time limits on learning the language etc... Mexico, what does your brother do?"

M: "Nothing. Well, my little brother sits around the house all day. Why?"

NE: "I thought you had two brothers or something and even a sister, right?"

Reluctantly, Mexico answers the question.

M: "The other one is in prison in Phoenix. What does that have to do with anything?"

NE: "Ok, I'm not tryin' to diss you, man, but I'm makin' a point. What's your mama do?"

M: "She takes care of my brother."

NE: "So your mama takes care of your brother and he's what, 20?"

M: "19."

NE: "So he's not working. He's 19. Your other brother is in jail, and youre here, right? What about your sister?"

M: "She's 17. Pregnant."

NE: "So really, you said that you had immigrated here when you were a lil kid and everyone was illegal, right?"

No answer.

NE: "So then your lil sis was born and that was the

ticket to stay in the country. Do the math. No one is contributing to the country at all except you. Nobody. Actually, your entire family, and I'm just talking math here, is an expenditure on our economy."

Mexico looked at him angrily but they were friends and he understood.

M: "Well, blacks are the same way!"

Bryce and Arkansas looked on.

NE: "Not as much though and there's one HUGE difference: We are citizens! So if we already have a population that must be enfranchised, so to speak, then why ADD to the number that requires special dispensation financially? It makes no sense."

M: "So whaddya mean, Notheast? (friendly pronunciation) You saying that you're any better than I am? Say, it bro-ham."

NE: "I'm gonna overlook that lil racial comment cuz we friends. I ain't no bro-ham, and I ain't denying there's unemployment in the black community. I'm just saying why INVITE problems into the country? We luv ya, man. You're one of us. But you know what I mean, right?"

B: "Hey, fellas, let's forget about all that stuff, ok?"

M: "He started it."

NE: "We're just talkin' and, besides, I'm the first to admit that there's a whole world of lazy ass bro-hams in my neighborhood. But I'm not one of them. All those lazy suckers that sit around and do nothin' but listen to music and get their head bad all day aint about shit. I'll be the very first one to admit that. But that ain't me, dog! Even worse, when they do make some money and get on TV with their music, everybody thinks that's good and they wanna do the same thing-all those stupid ass kids. Also, the whole world thinks that's America and it aint!"

A: "No one said it WAS you, Northeast. Just cuz you're black don't mean nothin'. Mexico's a lil defensive is all. But you're right. Any way it goes, we all need a lil help but we don't need to give away the farm to a bunch of foreigners. Has nothin to do with people as people but a matter of economics."

NE: "I hear dudes all the time say stuff like he gotta sell weed or rocks cuz he can't find a job. Man, there's work everywhere. And if they can't find work, why in the hell we lettin' in millions of foreigners? hey just some lazy motherfuckers, excuse my French. I borrowed money and got my degree. My cousin did too. But all the other guys around me are just hangin' out talkin bout getting' on some hoes. They aint about shit. And everyone thinks that is what America is these days-all that crap on TV talkin' about women and killin' and whatever. They are terrible role models and the world looks at people like them and think that's us. That's like a killin movie. People watch it but we aren't goin' around killin' folks. It makes me wanna puke!" (makes a vomiting motion)

M: "Me too."

B: "Yeah I know. I hate it."

A: "I don't see how y'all even listen to that shit."

Bryce smiled.

M: "There's nothing wrong with a little rap but Tejano is better!"

He threw his hands mockingly like gang members do talking in code.

Arkansas and Bryce laughed.

NE: "The music is Ok if it doesn't talk about killin' and doin' bad to women. That's for losers, man. A real man is gonna take care of his woman-not use her up. He aint gonna use up any woman cuz sooner or later she's gonna be SOMEone's wife!"

B: "I hear ya. I tell ya what gets me. The other day, there was this friggin pussy ass senator got up and said that we had lost the war!! Can you believe that crap?"

A: "I know it ! And Kerry had said that only losers join the military. Crap! Man that sucks. And he had the audacity to try and run for President-Commander-in-Chief of the military!. Can you imagine if he had gotten elected? Oh, crap! That would be like a faggot tryin' to be a daddy. How is he gonna teach his kid to be a real man? Impossible!"

All of them agreed. Brief silence for a minute. Then Bryce jumped in.

B: "When I was a kid, my father used to put it like this: There is always gonna be problems and bullies. Even though you keep to yourself, they're still gonna come. So you gotta just learn HOW to fight."

A: "That's right, Brycie."

NE: "Man, aint that the truth."

B: "In the old days, those friggin pussies would be left behind with the women huddling in the huts. After the other tribes would come and carry away the women and children-the women as sex slaves and the kids as friggin' houseboys, the men would come home from their hunt or whatever and then they'd have to go get them. Well, if some pussy ass didn't want to stick up for his tribe, even go get the helpless women and children, he'd stay in the hut whimpering in fear cuz he was a lil fraidy cat. He'd be stuck there with the old women and the old men who weren't even good enough to carry off. We're over here shedding our blood so some friggin radicals won't come on our soil again and some pansy ass is sitting up in Washington declaring 'We lost! 'We lost!' They needta run his ass outta town."

He spat on the ground.

A: "Damn, Brycie! You're a tough dude, man. But you're right. Definitely right!"

M: "Yo, man. I remember him-Reid or somethin' like that. They need to kick his ass outta office. He's a traitor."

B: "He aint no worse than that black general that retired and then started sayin' crap like he was against bein' here or somethin'. They need to take his pension away from him.

Everybody chimed in...

"I agree."

Chapter 11
The Pieces

In a deserted area outside of Baghdad, four Iraqis spoke in Arabic.

First, "There are many girls there, and they are the most precious to the collaborators. If we take them, we can pierce the heart of the infidel. They must be sacrificed for the greater purpose."

He grinned as he brushed his rotting teeth with a piece of wood shredded at the end.

Second, "Ahmed, make sure you have everything in order. We will strike them and cut them into a million pieces. My cousin worked there and he gave me the map of the area. There is a passageway that goes under the school."

Ahmed, the third man, looked on and nodded in agreement.

First, "Prepare yourself completely, for you have been entrusted with the future of our cause."

In the United States, a power meeting was in progress at 2:00 am with three Democratic senators.

"We have to focus on the rate of American deaths. The people hate to see that and it will discredit the President. That, way, it will open the way for a Democrat to be the next president. Besides, the poor people mainly care about their next paycheck. If we add some type of publicity to the mix like, uh, …(waves his hands in search of an answer) only rich people get tax breaks, that's like a double hit."

"Look…," the other senator broke in, "…I have a friend who can run that same message every hour on the hour. All we have to do is create doubt. Those poor son-of-a-bitches will eat it up."

Third man, "Hell, it worked in the Vietnam War. How much more now? That damn coward pulled out everyone."

Fourth man, "Yeah, and a million people died in Vietnam and Cambodia as a result."

He had spoken before he thought, actually, he had spoken ***what*** he thought-but before he could stop himself."

The other three stopped dead and turned and looked at him.

"Whose damn side are you on anyway?"

Fourth man, "Sorry, I wasn't thinking."

First man, "I suggest you pull your head outta your ass, son, cuz this is politics."

Second man, "Besides, I don't give a fuck what they found over there and the American public really has no idea about the link between Saddam and Syria. They got no idea 'bout the shipments back and forth. All they know is this: their kids may have to go. They'll do anything to keep that from happening…at least the women will. We need to run these ads during the day when lots of the women are at home. Plus, these friggin' spics are set to vote this time around, so are the fags and so are the blacks. We have to appeal to the money issue AND discredit the Republicans at the same time. Let's say the Republicans are gonna bring back the draft."

His face lit up.

Third man, "Perfect. I got an idea…."

The First man interrupted, "Sorry, Bill, let's feed that to a couple of talk shows. They'll eat that shit up."

Third man, "I was just saying that in order to appeal to the gays. We need to put in a separate issue like they could all get married or something'."

First man, "That's all well and fine but the American public in general hates all that faggot shit. They don't want to accept it-especially some faggots or lesbians livin' next door to 'em MARRIED, so we won't make like we're supporting it 100%-just that maybe they can get a national referendum of some kind. Let's not push our luck."

Second man, "That's true. Plus if we push that, we'll push away the Spic vote…er, uh, excuse me, (He spoke mockingly in a proper voice) HISPANIC vote."

They all laughed.

First man, "He's right. The Hispanics don't believe in that. Most of them are Catholics. That's why we need to simply say it's a woman's choice on abortion and leave it at that. Most of 'em are pretty friggin' stupid anyway and can't read and write, so if they know that we fully support killin' babies then they'll pull their vote. As is, the gays don't know what Catholic Hispanics believe and the Hispanics don't keep up on the possibility of gays getting married and that they would have to support them through taxes and social security -if they're legal that is. (He gestured wildly). Fuck, if those stupid asses even read the paper every now and then, we'd be done for. Hell, we'd be out of a job!"

Second man, "That's why we're here, Ted."

"Third man, grinning, "Well, hell, fellas, let's drink a drink to the ignorance of the public! They have no fuckin' idea that they can vote that shit outta existence. They aint gota let fags get married. Shit, it even makes me wanna vomit. But one thing is for sure-Our lil idea to put in liberal judges made us all millionaires, didn't it?" Then he laughed.

On the other side of Washington, D.C., a Republican power meeting had been in progressing for three hours.

The junior senator spoke directly to the President.

"Mr. President, we are definitely making progress in

the area. The troop surge has reduced violence, and the people are working with us now more than ever before."

Pres. Bush, "I know, but there has to be some way that we can make more progress. Yes, we are making progress day by day but the Iraqis need to step up to take more responsibility."

The President rubbed his head in anguish. The weight of the world was on his shoulders.

A junior Senator, "Mr. President, you have followed the right course in this, and inaction and tribal fighting on the part of the Iraqis is not your fault. They now have democracy. They no longer have to fear being gassed by Saddam Hussein. They don't have to fear the legitimacy of a dictator that could drag them out of their home any hour of the day or night, without due process. They no longer have to fear torture at the hands of their own government. The women don't have to worry that their sons or husbands or even daughters for that matter will be taken by the hands of policeman and never be heard from again."

A third person spoke, "We have other items to address, Mr. President. On the domestic front, we need to think about reelection platforms."

The President, "I am not signing off on same sex marriage. It is morally wrong, and I won't support that in any way!"

He was disgusted.

"Sir," the third man continued, "the democratic party

has steeped themselves in public concern that you're an exclusionist. They are appealing to the ignorance of the people by saying that if you reject same sex marriage that you are a 'hater,' as they say."

President, "Well, they can call me what they like, but I will not support same sex marriage nor will I support ripping a child from its mother's womb. These guys wanna talk about children's rights-even going so far as to address the idea that a kid can divorce his parents-but they ignore the fact that a child breathing in her stomach is alive."

Again, his disgust rang out through every word. It hung in the air like a cloud.

These were age old arguments between the parties. The Republican Party members knew what the tenets of the party were. Conversely, the disparate groups that made up the Democratic Party knew little of each other. Consequently the line between truth and reality was blurred by the Democrats. For their leaders, the target was to disseminate a little information regarding what they stood for, but not in its entirety. To do so, would pit the members against one another. This was a catch-all group. For the minorities, it meant more money in a welfare check-but they don't know that meant more taxes to pay for the immigrants that would be drawing form the same pot with food stamps, free medical care, and social security. For the gays, it meant the possibility of marriage, but the poor Christian blacks who voted democratic and who also supported open immigration had no idea that their 14 year old daughters would be able to get an abortion without their consent or even their knowledge and that the same immigrants they allowed in would come and take their jobs as a result of how they voted. Each sector of this catch-all group voted the democratic ballot because of only one small item that the Democratic party claimed it could get for them. They gave away their birthright for a bowl of porridge. They were the "me" generation of the second millennium.

The Democratic party was also a party of concealment. The Republican party was a party of revelation. The Republican administration would send people to get information to protect the country at large. The Democrats, however, were content with staying on the porch and letting someone else do the hard work. The Republicans sowed and the democrats wanted to reap. And so it had been.

The President continued, " And I know we're doing the right thing in Iraq. Our initial intelligence was right and Saddam had over a year to hide everything he had in his arsenal. He turned away weapons inspectors at every turn for a year. A whole year !! And we found the parts, the public forgot about that…'

"No. No, Sir. Those who know never forgot about that. The others are just listening to democrat controlled TV stations and newspapers that say 'No weapons were ever found.' The Republicans know because they read and watch other TV stations and listen to the radio. They know because they **want to** know!"

An army general joined in.

"Sir, I know that we underestimated the number of Al Qaeda that was actually in the country, Iraq, that is. But since then, we have made these amends and actually thwarted numerous attacks on American soil. In addition, the assorted tribal leaders have agreed to share the responsibilities in governmental elections. Intertribal fighting is at a minimum. Iraq is now free."

"You know, General, I agonize over this," said the President, rubbing his forehead.

"We all have, Sir. But may I speak off the record for a minute?"

"Of course."

"Sir, any people that would kill their next door neighbors by blowing themselves into a million pieces are capable of a whole lot more. This whole operation was done for the innocent people of Iraq as well as the safety of the American people. I don't have to remind you of the 4000 men, women, and children, and even babies that Saddam gassed nor of his torture chambers, nor of the tens of thousands of people that disappeared over his reign without a trace. Of course you already know. These terrorists enjoyed freedom under Saddam's rule, because they went from Syria to Iraq on covert missions. This was their agreement. The link between Iraq and Al Qaeda is a loose one because the name of AL Qaeda is a loose one to include terrorists that have raised themselves in arms against America. Furthermore, and this is really the bottom line, the last proof, so to speak: Anybody that would kill its own people for no reason at all, and I'm talking about Saddam or suicide bombers, or whatever, these people need to be taken out. Picture living right next to your neighbor for 20 years, and then when the good guys come to get you, blowing up your neighbor and his family, his old parents, and his young kids to fight the good guys. How does that fight America? It doesn't. That's like Rwanda all over again, but these people in Iraq have access to weapons and money and contacts- all over the world. They have the ability to kill wherever and whenever, and they do it in such a manner to kill as many as possible."

The President put up his hand in a motion to stop.

"Ok, General," the President said, "status report on enemy movement."

"Sir, the insurgents have moved north toward Erbil. In the past 24 hours, they have killed 63 civilians in three separate attacks. Intelligence indicates they want to destabilize the region of Kurdistan through attacks on Turkish bases in the north. This in turn would suggest that American involvement has unleashed the Kurdish radicals against Turkey."

"Ok, General, what's your assessment?"

"Mr. President, as we know, for the most part, the Kurdish minority has been the most prosperous and the north remains to be the safest area in the country. After their mass murder by Saddam's regime, the stragglers were relegated to the north of the country to be with the remaining population. When we came into the country, the Kurds set up a local currency that has prospered. They really have little reason to fight for a separate region like before. There are isolated instances of cross border raids against the Turks but these are mainly coming from inside the Turkish borders. The Al Qaeda insurgents have gone underground since the last bombing near Erbil which claimed 130 lives. We also have full cooperation from the Kurds to find the culprits. In addition, the past 48 hours have netted 140 insurgents in three separate areas immediately north of Baghdad. Four maps were found: Madrid, London, Bali, and Paris. This suggests future operations by Al Qaeda."

The President sat and looked at each individual in the room. He drew in a deep breath.

"You know, the idea of appeasement has never worked. When England took this approach with Hitler in 1939, it simply led to millions of lives being lost. Hitler continued westward and took Poland, France, The Netherlands, and then bombed London for 58 days straight. The people were living in the bunkers underground. Funny, France never did stand up at all through this whole thing. They lived through being taken over in WWII and still won't fight. They have to act like Germany and stay at home. Spain pulled its troops from the war on terror because their train was bombed in Madrid. Even after that. they were bombed again! People never learn, you give a bully your lunch money and he's definitely going to come back the next day. Alright then, men, let's make sure that Iraq stays free-just like Kuwait and Afghanistan. Millions of people around the world can go to bed tonight in peace because our men and women were American enough to stand up and fight for them."

Another senator in the room, "It must be done, Sir."

Chapter 12
Recognition

Aramex had hired some of the local girls to clean the apartments of the soldiers who lived in the neighborhoods. The idea was pretty simple and it worked. The soldiers were there to protect the people, gain their trust, and basically be their friends. Bryce had gotten a four bedroom apartment with three other soldiers in his unit. Bobby and Brycie were talking and running a couple of minutes late for work.

Bobby shifted on the couch.

"Brycie, man, I tell you. Sometimes I hate I even married her. She can be so rebellious at times."

"I know, Bobby, but you gotta hang in there. She's having a hard time, I imagine, at home with the baby all by herself. You know, a woman has to have her man with her."

Bryce's tone was encouraging, and he spoke form the

pain of his own heart, although no one knew it but him and his own girl.

"I tell you, I like Randi. She's so beautiful, and she keeps lookin' at me too."

"Bobby, that's not the way to go. That's a bad thing, bubba. Keep your head. Things'll get better with your wife. I'm sure of it."

"Ok, Bryce, I believe you. But a man can just take so much. I gotta go."

"I'm right behind you."

Bobby left and was met at the door by the two cleaning women. They were Iraqi girls in their early twenties.

Bryce came down the stairs and saw Sheikha. The second girl had already gone to the back bedroom and started cleaning.

Sheikha saw him and greeted with a mumble. In just a second, world passed between them. Bryce was hit by Mario Puzzo's proverbvial thunderbolt. For a second he was completely immobile and speechless. He stared at her, simply standing there, looking stupid, dumbfounded, and soaking in the loveliest woman he had ever seen in his life. She had a scarf on her head but it couldn't contain the hair that flowed down her back, wavy and light brown. Her eyebrows were like crowns over the darkest brown eyes that seemed to exude a sense of loveliness and hang in the air, capturing every molecule of oxygen that would love to float in their presence for even a second. These eyes were the light of her soul, her innocence and purity.

They told a story of a future devoted wife and obedient, loving daughter, who honored her parents and loved animals, and cried when no one was around, sometimes for no reason at all, waiting for her prince to come. He knew her world and her heart at first sight.

And she knew his.

She made her way onto the kitchen and began picking up. He followed her and began helping her. They exchanged cordialities. And day after day, she came. And day after day, he thought of her and she thought of him. She told him of her training to be a teacher. He told her of his plans to get a Master's degree.

✵   ✵   ✵

Weeks passed, and this was their routine. They both lived for these brief five minutes every day. It was clean. It was natural It was pure. But it was in the mouth of hell.

And on a certain day, she came. They talked and they laughed. When she laughed, she was funny and sexy. He loved her. And she loved him.

"Bryce, I have another word for you. I know the definition but I don't understand everything."

This was their routine. One word each day.

"O-b-e-d-i-e-n-t."

"Well, it means…."

"I know-to follow command. But how to say in a sentence?"

He thought for a second.

"Uh, the boy is obedient to his father."

He smiled.

She sat down on the kitchen chair (Their usual place was the kitchen, so she could talk while she worked.). She frowned.

"I don't like this word.."

Bryce chuckled.

"Why?"

"Well, it means that you have to do something you don't want to do it, right?"

"Yes, sometimes. What's wrong with that?"

She stammered for a second. She didn't want to say. And it hurt.

"Oh, forget. I ask different word tomorrow, OK?"

"OK. I'm going to work now."

He lingered for a second, and they stared at each other. They both lived for these minutes every day. Time passed. Weeks and weeks. He had the timing perfect. And it was proper. And it was real. But just outside those walls, the eyes of death roamed to and fro, looking for whom it might devour. And they knew it. Outside, they dare not even glance in the other's direction.

The dark of the room pervaded his flesh and sunk down in him like a stink. It was a smell of the eye that he couldn't seem to shake off. Night after night, Bryce would lay like this, his mind wandering through the past and into the future, creating scenarios that only the middle of the night could bring. But these dreams were conceived with eyes wide open. And he hurt, too. There was an emptiness in his heart that he had never experienced. Had he never seen her, he would have never experienced this ache. It was a dull throbbing ache. Like a toothache that is in the heart, one that thuds and throbs with an intermittence of variable types of pain. And he never knew how it would hurt on a certain day because he never knew exactly how much they could talk. When he practiced the certain conversation that he wanted for that day and had memorized the funniest thing to say with the perfect expression, she would be late or she had her own story. But he didn't care in the final analysis-as long as he could see her for just a mere second. To lay eyes on her was enough-until the next day.

This day she had been crying. He saw it. Her eyes were swollen and had dark circles that choked the life from her appearance.

His heart sank when he saw her. She wiped the counter diligently.

"What's wrong, Sheikha?"

His voice eased her and she felt her eyes brim with tears. She wanted to let it go like a dam bursting flooding the lowlands. And the pressure was almost the same. She turned away from him so he couldn't see her.

He had never touched her, but this time he grabbed her arm and turned her toward him gently. She turned in and and looked up at him and the dam burst. Tears literally shot from her eyes and she melted into him and just sobbed. He wrapped his strong arms around her and held her close. He could smell her hair and she clung to him for dear life, like a drowning child clings to a lifeguard.

Then she couldn't hold anything any longer and she broke down completely. With her tears and wails of heartache and pain and overwhelming helplessness, he held her, and for just a minute, they were both complete.

It was that spark that transcends all cultures, all ideas, and all taboos that are set to segregate peoples, especially male and female, one that was knitted in a moment of tender understanding and recognition: Heart recognizes heart-sometimes overriding the premise that spirit recognizes spirit. And it bound them inextricably forever-even unto today.

Chapter 13
The Answer

They were on patrol for two days. There had been violence between the Sunnis and the Shiites just north of the city. Intelligence indicated a local self-declared cleric (actually just an ex-butcher with a long beard) whom had previously vowed to kill all westerners had holed up in a village 20 kilometers outside of the city. The platoon had lain down for their shift and Bryce and Bobby stood guard.

It had been a long day. They had gone even further north before making their way back, distributing packs containing prayer rugs, tea, sugar, and a two kilos of rice. Most of the people had grown to trust the Americans by now, seeing that they brought peace and good will. The tide had turned against the insurgent extremists because too many attacks had been aimed at simply killing and creating chaos.

The law-abiding locals knew that the dirty little boy

who had lived on the edge of the village, the one they saw grow up, had grown into raping the local children, killing their own neighbors, and kidnapping in the name of religion. In their stupor to understand the overthrow of Saddam and Chemical Ali, , the blood of their families became their tutor. Slowly but surely, they saw the genuine willingness to help humanity progress walk through their streets carrying weapons of peace. And they began to work together with the US forces. They even saw the American anomalies who sinned against the locals, those who came to help but turned to illicit behavior come to justice by the hands of the American court martial. For this, the real American soldier was truly sorry. And the guilty parties will serve their days behind military bars-even though most agree they should serve their sentence at the end of a firing squad. Pluck out the eye if it offends you.

Bobby shifted his weight to his other foot. It was falling asleep on him.

"I'm telling you, Brycie, she told me that she's in love with another man. I really don't know what to do."

Bryce looked at him and his heart when out to him. Here is a guy at war and his wife is fooling around. This was the price a man paid for his country.

"Bryce, I don't know what I should do. You know, I got a little girl. What should I do, man?"

Bryce's past came rushing toward him and the words that his father had told were locked away for years, but all of a sudden, they were there.

"Bobby, you got to stay there. Somebody has to do the right thing. I know it hurts, Bobby, but you're a man. You can handle it."

"What do you mean, Bryce, let her cheat on me?"

"No, of course not, but right now, don't give her any ultimatums. Don't accept it but don't get nuts either. You gotta let her know how much you love her. That's the main thing she's looking for. She doesn't love anyone else. A woman cheats for three reasons: greed, need, or revenge. Most of the time a man cheats outta greed but a woman cheats outta need. Not that you don't meet her needs but she's alone, and the need she has is affection and that kinda stuff. The best thing to do is call her every single day."

"See, this is what I was saying the other day. Randi is crazy about me and she's always staring at me. And she's a million times better lookin' than my old lady."

"I know, but that's a losin' proposition. A guy can't be jumpin' back and forth between women. You can't go mixin it, Bobby. It aint right. Besides, I guarantee she'll melt if you simply take it back like before. I know Randi is cute and all, but you're bigger than that. You were made for one woman. And that's it. Did she sleep with him?"

"She said no."

"Well, it's pretty simple then. Repair it. Put in your time and do the work. You gotta just love her. No matter what, just love her. That's it-final analysis."

"How you know, Brycie?"

"My dad used to tell me crap when we were little. And I saw it too. It's too easy to walk away. And when you bring in someone else, it just complicates things. That won't cure anything. It'll just make it worse. I knew this guy, man. And his wife cheated on him with a guy she was working with. He stayed right there even though he wanted to kill someone. He could have done it too. But anyway, they eventually got back together and now they have a daughter. That little girl was definitely a love child. Actually the wife had even moved out. If they cheat, you don't have to put up with that. If they cheat or run off, you're free to get a divorce, of course. But my point is that he stayed there and forgave her and they got even better. Keep your head up, Bobby. And on down the road if they still screw up, then God will replace her with a better model of his own choosing. That's the key on all of it. That's what happened to my dad. He stayed there until we all grew up but things got even worse, and then God blessed him with someone else. But he left and **then** he met someone else. It has to be done in order. It all equals out, man."

"Yeah but guys sneak around all the time and never get caught."

"Bobby, that's just part of the picture, one little miniscule iota of the whole scenario. Doin' the right thing doesn't have anything at all to do with who's lookin' or if you get caught or what you get out of it. Do you believe in God?"

"Well, of course. I'm a Baptist. Once saved, always saved."

"Ok, then you know that you're here for a reason right?"

"Of course, we aren't just born willy- nilly. We all have a purpose."

"All right, check this out. Everyone has a gift. That gift is first of all given so that it will benefit others-not just ourselves. We were loved for the sake of our forefathers. We aren't likt eh opnly ones predestined to go to heaven or nothin' like that. Everyone has a chance at some point in their lives to know the way, the truth, and the life through Jesus but we that already know were chosen because way back in the beginning. We were children of promise… through the belief of Abraham. As a result, God said He would bless Abraham because Abraham simply believed Him. Then all those that believe that their sins are taken away are sons of Abraham and Isaac-not Esau or Ishmael because they are not sons of promise."

"Ok, I know all that Bryce. What are you getting at?"

"Let me finish and you'll see where you fit into all of it. It's really simple. Besides, I didn't say it. God said it. It's all in the Bible. So God said to Abraham, I'll give you a son because you are my friend and you believe what I say. That son was a son of promise because Abraham was already 86 years old and couldn't physically have kids. His wife got tired of waiting and then gave him Hagar his Egyptian maid. The wife was the weak one that didn't think she could have kids. So Abraham and the maid locked up to try and bring to pass what God had already promised. Their son was Ishmael, a bond child. God said cast him out because he is not a child of promise, and I'll raise up to him a great nation. The Arabs come from Ishmael. They are under the law. They reject as the Son of God, God come in the flesh. We are under the law of liberty. With Jesus, everything changed because the old law became nil and the law of faith that makes us righteous was established. No more slaughtering of animals or redundancy and repetition of form-even the Catholic forms are really unnecessary for salvation. When the church was established and with the advent of the Holy Spirit, the law was written in our hearts. There wasn't a new system of legalism enacted but the law of faith in the remission of sins through the blood of Jesus – God come in the flesh with no sin-and then our acceptance of Him makes us right with God. Jesus was the last sacrifice, like I say. He was killed on the cross. He rose after three days. Our resurrection in becoming a new man is the same as His when we accept Jesus as our savior…."

"Brycie, thanks for the history lesson but …what's the point?"

"Well, other than what the Bible said about other religions, such as 'accept no foundation other than Jesus Christ' and 'when people turn to Jesus, the veil is lifted' and 'where the Spirit of the Lord is, there is liberty,' this is it: with all of that, we were each given a specific task in this world, an assignment. And, once you figure out that you were called from the beginning of time, you also figure out that in the small daily realm such as the job, the family, the neighbor, you ought to know that God has a purpose for you too. That means the salvation of your wife and even of your little baby girl might depend on the decision you make regarding her near miss in the infidelity department. What you do now determines *her* future and the future of your *little girl* too. If God did all of that to give you life after death, then He has a plan for you here and now too. And when my mom cheated on my dad, he could have left but he didn't. He stayed there and taught me and my brother how to be men. Likewise, he had been a drinker. Seems all pretty bad but he changed his path and then we all saw him change before our eyes. He humbled himself before God and everything fell into place for him. I say it like that, but, in actuality, God breathed life into him and now the plan for his life has come to pass. Same with you, Bobby. You are called to be the priest of your home. They are under you, and you are responsible for the direction of those under your supervision. You can't make her obey you, but you can love and lead and be the best example possible. All the rest of it is dung, my friend. We were called to help these people here in this country. We were called to be moral ourselves though and let others live their own lives but also to protect those who can't protect themselves. Anyone else who says different has no knowledge about history. Actually it's impossible to be a real Christian and think otherwise. That's like having a gay bishop. It's impossible. The Bible says effeminates and homosexuals and murderers and drunkards and adulterers and fornicators will not enter the kingdom of heaven. And if they aren't goin' to heaven, they are sure goin' to hell. You can't drink the cup of demons and the cup of the Lord."

Bobby had been looking away, thinking about his position in the family, but he turned and looked at Bryce.

"What?"

"I said the Bible says all those guys are going to hell. Not only that, but it says if you once tasted the knowledge of Jesus and turn away, the end will be worse. So, that means you *can* backslide. It ain't, once you're saved, you're always saved. If you commit those sins and die, you'll die in those sins. Then you'll go straight to hell. That's it. Again, I didn't say it. God said that."

A tear made its way down Bobby's face-like a single, solitary thought that had inched its way to the surface. The tear was the only evidence the idea had been planted in his heart. He stared into the the stillness of the night and knew Bryce was right.

"What do I gotta do, Brycie?

"Bobby, there ain't nothin' to do except just accept Jesus. That's it. It's all a free gift. You can't pray your way into heaven or wash yourself clean enough or give money to get your way in. All these guys who say you're goin' to hell if you don't go to church are crazy. It's this. Believe that Jesus is the Son of God, God come in the flesh, that He died and rose after three days, and now lives. He took the hit for you, man, paid the price so you and me can be sinless and be with Him in eternity. We didn't do anything at all to deserve it. It is a free gift by your Maker. Just believe and ask forgiveness of your sins and that's all. After that, you walk and talk with Him daily and He will talk back. That's it."

"Yeah, but Brycie, I can do better than her. I mean Randi is even an officer. She makes good money. She likes me. She's educated. To be honest, she even looks better than the wife. She invited me over tonight."

"Let me tell you, Bobby. It's like this. Adultery is like a credit card. With a credit card, you trade in now for later. You might get something right this minute, but sooner or later, you're gonna pay for it. And the end is worse than the beginning. And *in the end*, at that exact minute that you're paying the price, all you got left is the past-then you look back and think, 'those were better days.' One main difference though, a credit card is good for an emergency -when you're in need. But there is no need that ever justifies adultery."

Those seeds of wisdom went deep into Bobby and produced results in him and his family for generations to come.

Family day was the best day of the week because free calls were available anywhere in the world. For the soldiers, this meant they could talk with every member of the family, from the youngest to the oldest. And for the family members at home, this meant they could have their own little family reunion while waiting for the call. As routine would have it, the room was crowded and each person seemed preoccupied with the business of home. That included not only "I love you's" but car payments, mortgages, school grades, advice for children, and everything that has occasion to nag throughout the week. But it was good. The nagging was the link to the real world, as long as it was minimal. A man (or woman) has to have his hand in things to feel needed. But he can't be needed so much to where it's overwhelming. Here, a second of distraction could lead in to eternity.

The line of twenty phones was filled and twenty or more people stood in each line, waiting and chatting quietly among themselves.

Arkansas made sure he knew about the bills, always the bills. But his wife was a competent woman. Strong. Independent. Had they lived a 100 years earlier, she would have been a physical match for him because of carrying water from the well and tending to the farm. But her strength was one of inner character. She had been on the farm all her life but now she had some modern conveniences…not the old life like before.

"The kids are ok," she said. You know the college wants a deposit on next year's dorm room."

"Ok. Ok," Arkansas said. "Tell Kenny to go to his recruiter and find out what to do. That's included in his deal. Plus, he should get his check before class starts. They ought to pay for his books too. It's full ride, Betty."

She drawled for a minute and answered, "Well, ok. Listen, Mark, don't worry about us. I'll get onto him about it."

There was a momentary silence. They had been married twenty years, and this was his life-coming and going. He never worried about anything getting done. But she knew just how much to give him to make him king from a distance. He was still in charge 8,000 miles away.

"Listen, Happy Anniversary in advance. I don't have to get you anything do I ?"

He was kidding, of course and she followed his lead.

"Oh, Mark, I forgot to tell you: I got another car yesterday…."

"Nice try, country girl. "

"Ha. Ha. Well, you started it. Keep your head down, boy. We love you. Mama is waiting for you when you get home."

Northeast spoke in whispers to avoid being the butt of any jokes.

"Look, little girl, you just keep my place warm, and I'll be home before you know it.

She spoke very softly and he loved it.

"I'll always keep your place warm, baby. You know, I am so thankful that God sent me a good man. I'll wait forever for my man!"

She did a little black girl inflection at the end of her claim. That said it all to him.

"Lookie here, baby, we gonna take that cruise we've been talkin' about once I get home. Your man loves you with all his heart."

"I know. Me too. I can't wait for you to be here."

Bobby was subdued but he ranged from hurt to angry. He had never been faced with infidelity. This was a thing that men usually just curse at and swear they are above-something *their* woman would never ever do. It's something men never tell their sons about. He recalled the conversation with Bryce while on patrol.

"Remember, you attract what you put out. You act like a whore, you attract a whore. You be good man, you'll attract a good woman. Remember how it was at the beginning and take it back. A woman is like a scared doe that wanders into your backyard. You can't rush it or else it'll run off. Take your time. Be nice. Let her trust you. Let her know that you don't want anything *from* her but everything *for* her. After a while, she'll come right up to you."

Bobby tried to speak quietly but his anger level made his voice fluctuate.

She sat and listened to him. His three minute limit

had lapsed twenty minutes earlier but everyone in line knew the problems that everyone else had. This was family, and they looked the other way.

"Sweetheart, I just don't understand how you could do this to me. But I want you to know this. I love you, and I forgive you. I am sorry that I must be away. I put aside all my feelings here and now so that you and I can move on with our lives. We have a child. You know, baby, I'm all yours and I willingly give myself for you all the days of my life."

He took away all the selfish justification and every reason that had exalted itself against faithfulness to her.

She melted and started crying

" Bobby, I am sooo sorry. I broke it off. Bobby, I swear I never let him touch me. I was weak. Please please please forgive me. I love you. I love you. I promise, I'll go to church on Sunday. I am pure for you, my Bobby! Just lead and I'll follow."

Maria spoke softly to her man. Things were a little strained between them. He was quiet and she wanted to know why. His mind was on Sheikha.

"Brycie, I don't know why you're so quiet. Is something wrong?"

"Naw, girl. I just gotta lotta stuff on my mind. Plus, I'm tired."

"Honey, you know your little Mexican flower is right here for you, right?"

He smiled. She was an excellent girl and they were

childhood sweethearts. He felt guilty because he had always had a pure heart toward her, never defiled her, always treated her like a lady. But he had never been hit by the thunderbolt either…at least not since Maria, and that was almost half his life ago.

He and Maria had grown up together. Together almost every day since they were 15 years old. That was a lot of history. It wasn't an automatic love like with Sheikha. They were kids. It *was* an automatic attraction though. But it grew and grew. When he was a young boy with pimples on his face, they were best friends. They talked about everything under the sun. They believed alike. They were inseparable. They knew each other's thoughts and moods and feelings and deepest fears. She was the most beautiful girl in the world to him…at least until Sheikha. But he had no illicit thoughts toward her either. He had clean thoughts all the way around.

Their conversation had been forced.

"Brycie, I can't wait to see you. Mama keeps asking me about a grandbaby. I said, 'Mama, we aren't even married yet.' What do you think, Brycie? Any ideas on that?"

Silence.

"Bryce, why are you so quiet?"

Pause.

"Ah, nothin' but stuff here is all."

She knew better. Some guys just can't divide the heart. Though he had never touched Sheikha, he loved her, and she loved him. The both knew it. Sometimes, it never has to be said. Sometimes, nature just takes its course. But honor is a strange thing. It's a stop gap. Its stops infidelity and deceit. But when there is no infidelity and there is no deceit, it stops communication.

"Brycie, I feel like there's something you're not telling me. Tell me you love me. Tell me I'm the only girl in the whole wide world for you. "

"C'mon, Maria, uh…"

She hesitated and he heard a sniffle across the phone, but she was a strong girl.

"Brycie, I am all yours. I will sit here and wait til the end of time if I have to. I know one thing and one thing only: God made me for you. I'm yours. No one has ever touched me. No one will ever touch me because I belong to Brycie. I don't care if this war takes twenty years, I will be here waiting for my Brycie when it's all over. So I am here. We all love you and we're thinking of you every day. Don't worry about me. OK?"

"I know, preciosa. You know what, you're like the best thing that ever happened to me."

"Me too, mi mulatto. I always pray that Jesus will keep you and watch over you. You are always always in my prayers. And when you come home, we gonna get married and have a baby and buy a house and I'm gonna cook for my husband."

She liked to talk about it and he liked to hear about it.

"Listen, Maria, I gotta go. I got duty in a few."

"Ok, I love you with all my heart. Brycie, tell me you love me. And that you are coming home to mamasita. I'm gonna wait for you all my life til you come back to me. I am all yours!"

"I love you, and I'm coming home to my lil Latina"

As he walked away, his heart sunk. He was in between his rock Maria and the hard place Sheikha. To Bryce, even being attracted to another girl was a big thing. Attraction was ok but being alone with a girl, no matter how innocent, was pushing the safety zone. Even though he would never in a million years compromise the values of Sheikha, he loved her and she loved him. It was just there.

Bryce, Northeast, and Arkansas made their way into town. It was a nice day, and everyone was in a jovial mood. They parked and walked a block toward their duty stations. Arkansas picked at Bryce.

" Hey Brycie, you call that little Tejana of yours?"

"You never mind about me and my Tejana, country boy. How's the family?"

"Ah, they're ok. Kenny will be starting college here pretty quick. He may be over here with us before too long. Except he'll be an officer. He'll be telling his old man what to do. "

They all laughed.

"How about you, northeast? How's the little lady?"

"Ah, she's spending money as usual. She's wanting to do a cruise or something on leave. She's ok though. Her little brother started the university. I guess he's keeping his head down and nose clean. I'm happy about that. He had his hard time, you know."

They heard a bell across the street and hundreds of girls started to pour out of the building. The three men stood where they were and let the girls pour into the street and make their way around them.

A blast tore through the building and the top half of the school exploded. Debris rained everywhere. Dozens of girls in the street were hit and fell to the ground instantly. Bryce ran toward the building and saw countless young ladies bloodied and maimed. There was screaming and screeching and howling everywhere.

Scores of girls ran into the streets. Even more ran from the building. Fire engulfed the top half of the building that remained intact. Bryce was a hundred yards from the school's main entrance with Arkansas and Northeast directly behind him. Girls ran continued to run from the building, and the more there were, the bloodier they were. Some came out with their arms blown off. Others had pieces of metal or glass stuck in their faces.

A second blast erupted, and it collapsed the main entrance. Seconds ticked away and the whole building caved in, trapping all survivors. People from every direction ran toward the building. There was only chaos. Local shopkeepers and parents began to help who they could. Men ripped their own shirts off their backs and made tourniquets. At the top of an adjoining hill, a group of four looked at the confusion and laughed.

Hundreds of young girls lay in the street, over balconies, across steps, bleeding, crying, moaning, and dying. These young and innocent children whom had never done one thing wrong would never know the basic joy of being a woman. Some lost their eyes, some their hands or fingers or toes or legs. Those were the lucky ones.

In the U.S., a democratic senator derided America's involvement in the war on terror. "There is no evidence of weapons of mass destruction. We must withdraw immediately...."

Arkansas ran to where the main entrance had been. He could hear screaming from under the debris. He pulled back two slabs of concrete from atop a young girl. Her head was partially caved in and she had blood all over her face. She was whimpering. Northeast ran to his side and they lifted one last slab off of her and pulled her from from the rubble. They worked frantically to help as many as possible as fast as possible.

Marines started to pour in from everywhere. They all started to coordinate. Body after body lay motionless, some only in pieces. Northeast came on a young girl who had been talking on the cell phone with her mother about a party. He found only the upper half of her body. He looked at her eyes and saw the innocence. She still clutched the cell phone in her hand. He immediately vomited.

Disregarding his own safety, another marine made his way into the shell of the building where some of the walls remained. People warned him to stay away but he could hear cries from where he was heading. He found a girl in the corner, calling and calling. Her legs were crushed under the concrete. He started digging tirelessly. As he dug he was strengthened. He lifted numerous pieces. Suddenly, the wall behind him fell inward, directly on top of the marine. A monstrous piece hit him directly on the head and killed him instantly.

Wails of lament shrouded the air for days to come.

In the U.S., a democrat senator who believed in abortion and gay marriage derided America's involvement in the war on terror. "There is no evidence of weapons of mass destruction. We must withdraw immediately…."

The death toll that day was 232-including 211 children: all GIRLS.

Chapter 14
Discovery

Several days passed and the girls never came by to clean Bryce's house. The men were worried about them but soon Sheikha's friend came alone. Bryce looked at her and offered his condolences.

She had lost six friends in the explosion. One was engaged.

"Where's Sheikha?"

His heart was pounding, and his stomach was queasy.

"She's Ok. Don't worry about her. But her brother is making her stay home for now. Not because of the blast but he doesn't want her here. "

"Why! Why? What's the problem here? She's very safe."

"I know. I know. But he has given her away to be married."

Bryce felt like someone slugged him in the stomach. His legs got weak and his throat had absolutely no moisture at all. His tongue felt swollen and he could hardly speak.

"She doesn't want to get married but they're making her marry her cousin from the province. The cousin hates all Americans and her brother thought it best for her not to return here. It's too dangerous."

She looked away as if to close the conversation.

"But, why is it dangerous? We won't hurt her. What's the matter?"

The girl never looked up and kept wiping.

He grabbed her arm and she turned and looked at him.

"Sheikha told me about you. She said that she feels love in her heart like she never felt before. She also thinks that maybe her brother read her diary." "But, but, where is she now?"

"Bryce, let it go now. "

But, Shaima, please tell me. "

"You can't talk to her because there are eyes everywhere. But I know that if she can just see you one more time, she will feel complete. This she told me. She is working at the old souk on Bandar street. "

That night he made his way there. From a distance, he could see her. She was the most beautiful girl he had ever seen and she exuded a warmth and femininity exclusive to her Sheika-ness. He recognized her before she even turned around. She was wrapping something for a customer. She turned and caught him staring at her from behind another counter of goods. People were milling about and no one seemed to pay any attention although everyone was aware of his presence. No one looked but everyone saw. Furtive glances were everywhere but nothing obvious. Yet he felt the tension. They locked eyes for only a couple of seconds and it was worth a month's conversation. She knew why he was there. Her heart leapt inside of her. Conscious of the surroundings, they spoke no words and gave no smile. The eyes said it all.

The next day he was on patrol with Bobby. They were in the street and the merchants greeted them as they walked by. They were known and trusted among the people. The locals knew their sacrifice and welcomed the peace they brought.

As they neared the end of the block, Bryce caught a man looking at him hard from across the street. He didn't just look but he stared. It was aimed at Bryce, a piercing stare that confronted him man to man. Bryce stopped dead and turned. Any other place, any other time, and he would have gone across the street and rolled up his sleeves. They stood there for a about eight seconds. Bobby kept walking. It was personal, and Bryce knew it. He let Bobby go so he could handle on a personal level. Bryce edged toward the center of the street as he waited for cars passing by. When it was clear to cross, the man had vanished.

Chapter 15
Cleaned

Stanley couldn't figure out how he had gotten roped into this one. Charles was at home, drinking as usual. Stanley had begun to feel that his whole life was a mistake. He just couldn't figure out why things never turned out right. He felt out of place and dirty. Not only that, but his heart seemed to condemn him. There was no way of escaping it-not sex, not getting high, not entertainment. Deep inside, he felt like he had no purpose and as if one day simply ran into the next, without end, but just a continuation of existence. This in and of itself was bad enough, but on top of that, he was beaten up frequently. There was just no light at the end of the tunnel.

People were so friendly to him as he came in with his mother. He had grown up here many years before, but it had been an equal number of years since he had been inside the sanctuary. And it was as if each member in this small congregation made an effort to welcome him and shake his hand. He felt truly at ease. His mother made her way to sit at her normal spot near the front but he pulled her back.

"Mama, I don't want to sit up front," He whispered, "People are gonna be starin' at us."

"Well, that's alright, honey. We can sit wherever you want."

He grabbed the second pew from the back and on the corner so he could make a fast getaway if need be.

He felt uneasy because he knew that they knew he was gay. But he didn't feel condemned at all. After a round or two of singing, the preacher began his sermon, reading from Hebrews 3.

"Therefore, as the Holy Spirit says, 'Today, when you hear His voice, do not harden your heart as in the Rebellion, as on the day of testing in the wilderness, where your fathers put me to the test and saw my works for forty years. Therefore, I was provoked with that generation, and said, 'They always go astray in their hearts; they have not known my ways,' As I swore in my wrath, 'They shall never enter into my rest.'"

In an instant, things began to make sense to Stanley. He had hardened his heart years ago, swearing to himself that he would go his own way, reasoning that he had the right to do what made him happy. But he listened more and his heart began to open up as he heard. It was as if a holy presence came to him personally. Just the exact same way that he knew evil existed, the same evil that you can feel, a tangible presence that rips at you and makes you want to run, there was here and now just the exact opposite and it came directly to him and spoke to his heart and melted away every single piece of bitterness. He was cleansed in an instant. He couldn't walk away from it, couldn't reason with it. His heart completely understood.

"…and with whom was He provoked forty years? Was it not those who sinned, whose bodies fell in the wilderness? And to whom did he swear that they should never enter into His rest, but to those who were disobedient? So we see that they were unable to enter into rest because of unbelief."

The pastor stopped reading and looked with loving eyes into the congregation. "The rest, my friends, is the relationship with God thru Jesus and his blood that comes through simply believing God and what He said. When I was a little boy, I didn't know what my Papa said was for my good and never saw behind the scenes of things. After I became a Papa, I saw first-hand how the things that I did were for the benefit of my children, although they couldn't see it at the time. When they asked me for this or that, and when I said OK, they became impatient at times and doubted me. But I did my best to see that I kept my word to them. How much more will our heavenly Father do the same? He is able to do all that he promised. But we have an obligation too. It's not a one sided affair."

Stanley felt a conviction come over him, one born through love. He felt a Godly grief overtake him and grab his heartstrings and pull. He heard an inaudible voice whisper into his spirit, " I love you…."

His heart melted and he began to weep. No one looked but everyone saw.

The choir started to sing very gently as the preacher continued to talk.

"Just as I am without one plea…."

"Come," he heard in his spirit. "Come unto me… where there is life."

The preacher took out a handkerchief and wiped his face,

"Listen, that gentle tugging that you feel is the Holy Spirit talking to you. Don't be afraid. Give in because that is the loving Holy Spirit that is sent by Jesus our Lord and proceeds from the Father to call unto Him those whom He chooses. Give into it. Don't harden your heart."

Stanley couldn't control his emotions. He had been moved by the love of Jesus and realized the holy presence that surrounded him. For the first time ever, he experienced the reality of God.

"Go on and get up. Just come down here right now and your whole life will change. He has called you today for a purpose, and we never know the last time He will call us. Tomorrow is never promised to us. Even His children fell in the wilderness because they hardened their heart. They sat down to eat and drink and rose up to play. 23,000 fell that day. The Holy Spirit is calling you now."

With that, Stanley got up and went to the alter and knelt. The elders of the church gathered and laid hands on him. He confessed his sins and accepted Jesus as his Lord and savior. As he was kneeling, he could literally feel a burden removed from him and his heart was instantly cleaned.

Across town, Charles sat drinking heavily. His test results had returned positive several days earlier, and he had been in a drunken stupor ever since. He cried intermittently and pitied himself without end. His logic had drained him and there was nothing left. His curses, self justification, and energy waned right along with the bottle of whiskey on the table. He threw out the ice from his glass. He sat in a blank stare for about thirty minutes and wondered who would lament him. Then he took a fistful of sleeping pills and chugged about eight ounces of hard liquor. He slipped away and then vomited. Five short convulsions later, he was gone. But his troubles had only just begun.

Charles' old psychotherapist sat on the couch and soaked up TV. She had grown old since she had seen Charles last. She gained fifty pounds and had health problems. She was still a slut and addicted to painkillers. She had been through two husbands since then but couldn't figure out why-only the fact that she was much smarter than they were and they had felt intimidated by her. She had been caught in adultery by her last husband and that was that. The first one had always turned a blind eye. Now she was fat, ugly, slutty, addicted, and nasty, but she still had her Ph.D.-and a *dead* ex-patient-the one she said should be allowed to explore *his* feelings.

Several days later, Charles' father said to the mother, "Maybe we were wrong in allowing Charles to dress up like a little girl."

"How was I supposed to know he would get confused? It's not my fault! " she retorted in self defense.

They both had **to take the guilt** to their grave because they were too weak **to take control.**

Mikie and Jamal often slithered through the streets of Houston, ducking and diving. And today was no different.

"Pass the blunt, nigga. Fire it up or somethin."

"Hey, yo, Jamal. There's a fuckin pig right behind ya."

"Aw, mutherfucker. Damn."

Mikie tossed his blunt under the seat. It rolled and lodged under the carpet, never to be found again.

The police immediately ordered the two to exit the car slowly.

One patted dwon both men.

"Why did you stop us, man?" Jamal said.

"Sir, you didn't come to a complete stop at the light."

Jamal was perturbed and his voice gave him away.

"Y'all aint got nothing better to do than to stop a brotha while he tryin to go to work."

"Sir, are there any weapons in the car?"

The other officer found a gun under the seat.

"Hey Rick, look what I found!"

The police officer held up the gun.

"That's not mine."

"Sir, you're under arrest for carrying a concealed weapon without a permit and a having a loaded firearm in your vehicle."

Jamal never made bail, and he did a year minus a day in the county jail. Mikie counted his blessings and got a job for $8 per hour. Mikie's days of slumming were over. Eventually he married and had a family. He taught his two sons a better way to live.

Chapter 16
Sheikha

Sheikha's brother was an austere man, self-inflated, with a false sense of importance and leadership. He carried the outdated, sense of moral superiority that men were honored with innate morality, intellectual prowess, and direction for every member of the family. With these ideas, he ruled with an iron hand, and every single male looked the other direction. What happened behind closed doors and within the family was confidential, warranted, and mostly just.

Sheikha had dressed quickly for her brother had ordered her readiness the night before. Their trip to the country was mandatory for her impending nuptials. Arrangements were to be made for the post wedding celebration. Therefore, she was to approve of the location, although this was not customary.

They made their way through numerous checkpoints and on into the lower mountainous region southwest of the city. It was hot and the car had no air conditioning. The brother had water in the trunk and they talked and laughed, recalling the good ole days of their youth. The conversation experienced repeated lulls because they never were too close, but still they were blood.

During these periods of silence, she thought of Bryce, her future, and her past. She was so helpless, almost like a piece of meat ordered about for the pleasure of someone else. She only ever had two things she wanted-to sit in the classroom and to talk with Bryce. Both times, she felt alive. But nothing ever compared to the time with Bryce. It was as if her whole life of misery and boredom was worth the small amount of time she had spent with him. Nothing in her life had ever been cleaner and more natural than the love she felt for Bryce. And now she would never see him again. She fought back the tears as they drove.

They pulled into an old farm and stopped. Sheikha felt confused and uneasy. It seemed an odd place to have a party.

"Why are we stopping here? We can't have a celebration here. "

He perceived the nervousness in her voice.

"Relax, Sheikha. Come in and we will get something to drink. I must check the engine and fill the radiator with water. Go into the house. I'm right behind you. The door is open. It's empty because Saad is down with the sheep."

She went to the door and it was ajar. She slowly opened the door and peeked in."

"Marhaba (hi), marhaba."

She stepped into the threshold and stood, listening. She could hear her brother approaching from behind her and felt safe.

Instantly she was grabbed from behind and her throat was slit in one fluid motion.

Several days went by and Bryce worried about Sheikha. He went back to the market several times but saw no sign of her. He fought the fatigue and emotions that went with the deep cut of love. Those feelings could be his downfall if he slipped for just a second.

The day slipped away and he made his way home with Bobby. He got into his room, kicked off his boots, and put his pistol under his pillow. He felt something fuzzy and wet. His finger had blood on it. He pulled back the pillow. Sheikha's hair.

Chapter 17

"Supposed to be here"

Arkansas fidgeted as he talked with his wife. Patrol was in a minute and he always had a talk before he went out-anytime, night or day. That was the rule.

Betty spoke to him like always and he listened to her. He knew a man has to listen to his woman just like she has to listen to him. Likewise, the both knew when to stop talking.

"Mark, I know, we know, you have to be there. We know that the fate of the world actually depends on you and people just like you. We are sooo proud of you."

"Thanks, baby. I know it gets a lil lonely around the house all by yourself. Just hang in there and I'll be home pretty soon. After all, just another two years and I'll be able to retire."

"Ooh, I know it. But listen, not many people are willing to stand up and fight. Most of 'em wanna sit around and complain and talk about freedom but they don't wanna pay for it. I'm so proud of my man cuz he's willing to be a real man and fight for the safety of us here and even for people he doesn't even know. Think about all those poor little girls who got killed in that school. What kinda animals would do something like that?"

"Huh, the same ones who already came over to the U.S. and did it to us."

"Mark, I know they spit on your daddy when he came back from Vietnam but look how many people were saved there and think how many were murdered when we left Vietnam. The Khmer Rouge killed at least a million because we left. Myanmar is a direct result of that and they're even killing Buddhist priests of all the people in the world. Those stupid idiots look and say 'well, there's no problem in Vietnam now' but they have no idea that's why things are like they are. Mark, if it weren't for you and a President who has enough guts to go out and get the bad guys - who ALREADY came here and murdered us with no provocation whatsoever - then half the world would be under bondage at this very minute."

Mark felt a lift in his soul. This is why he loved her so much-she simply knew.

"Yeah, well…"

"Mark, cowards have been against standing up and doing the right thing since the beginning of time. Just think, if people like you and President Bush hadn't stood up and done the right thing, then we would have never existed. France would be German. The UK would have been bombed into oblivion. England would either no longer exist or they'd be German as well. They are our closest friend because they know the difference between lying down and quitting and standing up and fighting. The Philippines would be Japanese. All of the Pacific would be speaking Japanese if we hadn't gone and fought. And we were attacked on 911 exactly like the Japanese attacked Pearl Harbor. There's not one iota of difference. Not at all. And even though weak countries and weakling people like France turn on us and would rather sit around and be gay and live decadent lifestyles, someone has to stand up-someone. That's you. It's all kinda strange that people who believe in filthy lifestyles and have no regard for morality ally themselves with communists and fascists like Germany to veto any type of action against terrorists. In fact, just recently France and China and Germany all stood together against any sanctions on Mugabe. Mark, the world depends on you. History has shown it. We already have proven it time and time again. But countries like France are like whores who sleep with their husbands and then bring other men into the bed after he's gone to work. They talk out of both sides of their mouth. That's why the democrats who say 'No war, No war' also believe in gay marriage and abortion on demand, even for 15 year old little girls. They're whores who simply go to the highest bidder. Whatever they can get is wherever they go and buy into whatever is being sold. Think of the results of that. I don't want to pay for health care so that two men or two women can live together and be married next door and I have to pay for it. "

"Me neither."

"A vote for them ends up with adultery in the white house-ha-in the oval office! It makes me want to vomit."

"Betty, I gotta go...."

Chapter 18
Firefight

Bryce, Bobby, Northeast, Arkansas and Mexico made their way through a small village 20 clicks north of the city. This was routine.

Bobby was on point, ahead of the group about 40 yards. There were a couple of concrete houses on each side of the narrow dirt road and a hill on the right another 15 yards.

A woman in an obaya with her face uncovered stood over a baby screaming and wailing. The squad immediately went on alert and fanned out. Bobby made his way to the woman and edged his way toward her. She had tears all over her face and snot running from her nose. She turned and screamed at Bobby and waved frantically.

Bobby came to her side and bent over the child.

Bryce saw from a distance and yelled, "No!"

A solitary shot cracked out and exploded Bobby's right temple. He slumped over the bay and the woman dropped down hollering frantically. At their left rear, an AL Qaeda fired from the corner of one of the houses. He sprayed the side of Bryce and Northeast. They both ran to the nearest house, same side of the street. They returned fire. Across the dirt road, Mexico and Arkansas ducked under the overhang of a house. They opened fire at the AL Qaeda. He dropped but another came, then two. Northeast was caught in the neck. He fell. Bryce opened up and ran back to him, grabbed Northeast by the collar, and dragged him into the house closest. He knelt at the door and opened up, emptied his clip, and reloaded. From the other end of that same house, two more men inched forward and around the corner. Mexico and Arkansas saw them from across the street and rained fire. Two went down, and two more ran to the back of the house. Bryce was trapped inside with Northeast. Mexico pulled a grenade and stood up to throw, as he did, he was shot in the chest. He threw it as hard as he could and to the corner where the first several terrorists had come. It hit all of them, dead in the center. Two arms fell into the street. Arkansas grabbed Mexico and pulled him into the house. Bryce was silent across the street but Arkansas could see him at the door. He also knew that three men were in back of the house.

Mexico looked up at Arkansas, "Hey country boy, I'm supposed to be helpin' you."

Arkansas laughed, "Yeah right, we don't need no more Mexicans."

Mexico smiled through his pain and then grinned weakly.

"I'm not Mexican. I'm American."

They smiled at each other.

Arkansas called to Bryce.

"Brycie, whatcha gonna do?"

"I gotta get round the back. Cover me."

Northeast was bleeding profusely. Bryce pulled him into a corner and looked thru the house. He found a piece of steel and laid it over the top of Northeast who was drifting in and out of consciousness.

He heard gunshots outside and ran to the door. Four men were running into the house across the street. He raised his machine gun and tore away.

Kkkkkkkkkkkkkkkkkkkkkkkk!

Then short, controlled bursts. Two went down and two made it thru the door. Arkansas stood just inside of the door and fired on them as they came through. He hit both but one unloaded as he went down, rattling off a burst of fire straight into Arkansas. Blood spurted everywhere. He went down and Mexico fired one shot into the other's head.

Bryce ran across the street but came under fire from the corner of the house where he had been. He turned and fell to the ground. He squeezed several times and all of them fell-four.

Then there was a giant explosion that ripped through one of the houses.

Darkness.

Silence.

Death.

Chapter 19

She sat and waited. She moved and situated herself over and again and resituated herself. She was nervous. No food. No drink. She felt a little sick at the stomach.

She listened to Garth Brooks sing if tomorrows never came.

Her heart sunk and then it lifted and then she had to go to the bathroom and then she felt a little at ease and then and then.

Finally she decided she would just rest and let the time pass.

She drifted off to nothingness.

Then she felt a nudge.

A deep voice awakened her.

"Miss, I'm sorry you can't sleep here."

She managed to get her eyes open and then realized where she was.

She looked up and saw the old familiar smile of Bryce.

She jumped up and hugged him and squeezed ever so tightly and then began to rattle on....

A loud speaker in the distance, "Flight 486 to Dallas now boarding."